Baby Steps

Lisa R. Schoolcraft

Baby Steps

Lisa R. Schoolcraft

Printed in the United States of America

First Printing, 2022

ISBN-978-1733970952

Publisher: Schoolcraft Ink LLC

Visit the author's website at www.schoolcraftink.com

Table of Contents

Chapter 1 1

Chapter 2 10

Chapter 3 23

Chapter 4 27

Chapter 5 37

Chapter 6 48

Chapter 7 59

Chapter 8 69

Chapter 9 79

Chapter 10 89

Chapter 11 98

Chapter 12 111

Chapter 13 117

Chapter 14 124

Chapter 15 134

Chapter 16 144

Chapter 17 154

Chapter 18 165

Chapter 1

Ravyn Shaw awoke to the sound of a baby crying through the baby monitor. Beside her in the bed, her husband, Marc Linder slept soundly. She could hear him snoring.

Ravyn rolled over and planted her feet on the bedroom floor and bleary-eyed, went to breastfeed her daughter. Ravyn's breasts ached. Her lower back ached. She ached. She was tired all the time.

She entered the nursery and went to her daughter, not turning on any lights. A dim University of Missouri night light illuminated the crib.

"Hey baby girl," Ravyn whispered. "Are you hungry, or are you wet?"

Ravyn felt the edge of her daughter's diaper and didn't feel any wetness. "Hungry then."

She lifted her daughter out of her crib, careful to cradle her neck and sat in a rocking chair her parents had given her the day Harper Shaw Linder had been born. She pulled Harper to her breast and mother and daughter sat in the quiet nursery rocking gently.

Ravyn tried to move her daughter to her other breast, but she was asleep, a little milk drooling out of her bow-shaped mouth. Harper did a little smacking, as if she were still breastfeeding, but Ravyn knew she would sleep soundly for another few hours.

Ravyn kissed her daughter lightly on the forehead, then laid her daughter back in the crib, careful to put her on her back. "Goodnight, baby girl," she whispered.

Ravyn padded back into the master bedroom and saw her husband Marc had rolled over, taking nearly the whole bed. "Hey," she said, nudging him on the shoulder. Marc didn't move. "Hey!" she said more loudly.

"What? What? Is it Harper?" Marc asked, startled awake.

"No, it's you. You're in my spot."

"Sorry," he said sleepily. "Were you up feeding Harper?"

Ravyn slid back into bed. It was warm where Marc had been sleeping, so she wasn't too mad at him. "Yes. She was crying. She was hungry."

"She was crying?"

"Marc, I know you are a heavy sleeper, but it worries me you don't even hear her crying."

"I'm sorry," he said. Then he rolled over and fell back asleep.

Ravyn tried to go back to sleep but couldn't get comfortable. Her breasts felt heavy. She knew she should get up and pump the breast Harper hadn't nursed.

Ravyn sighed heavily and got out of bed, walking into the kitchen, and turning on the light under the microwave. It gave off a softer light than the overhead kitchen light.

She reached into the drain board where her recently washed breast pump had dried. She got a clean bottle and began to pump. When it was full, she stopped, capped the bottle, and put it in the refrigerator. She wiped her breast and washed the pump, replacing it in the drainboard.

Ravyn wandered back to the bedroom and finally fell asleep. She was sleeping soundly when she heard Harper wail.

Marc popped his head up off the pillow. "That I heard. I'll get her."

Marc and Ravyn had married in July 2015 when Ravyn discovered she was pregnant. The couple had been engaged but moved up the wedding. Harper arrived shortly after Valentine's Day 2016 thanks in no small part to Marc's brother Bruce.

Bruce Linder is a recovering alcoholic and addict, and Marc has not held his brother in high esteem, even though Bruce practically saved Marc and Ravyn's outdoor wedding tent from going up in flames.

Bruce's quick thinking with a nearby garden hose had doused the fire even before the fire department had arrived.

A week before Harper's due date of February 18, Ravyn was still confined to bed rest and miserable. She couldn't get comfortable and nearly always had to pee.

Ravyn's pregnancy had gone well until the final eight weeks when her OB/GYN had raised concerns that the baby wasn't gaining weight. Dr. Brenda Watkins had ordered Ravyn to bed rest, laying on her left side until the baby was born.

Ravyn called Marc crying.

"My doctor has put me on bed rest! I can't work!"

Baby Steps

"What? Why? Is the baby ok?" He asked, concerned.

"The doctor is concerned she's not gaining weight."

"Oh. What can I do? Can you work from home? I can go to your office and get your files. Can you use your laptop at home?"

Ravyn stopped crying when she thought Marc might be right. She might be able to work from home.

Ravyn Shaw was the managing editor of *Cleopatra* magazine, a lifestyle magazine in Atlanta, focused on fashion, design, restaurants, cool vacation spots and other trends. She'd been working at the magazine for a little over two years.

Before that she'd been a freelance writer. It was how she and Marc met.

At the time, he was CEO of LindMark Enterprises Inc. She was to do a profile on him as one of Atlanta Trends "Rising Stars" in the tech industry. Their professional relationship got off to a rocky start. When the relationship turned personal, Marc's former lover and publicist Laura Lucas, had driven them apart.

Eventually, they both realized they loved each other, moved in together and got engaged.

Marc had since sold a majority interest in his company to Black Kat Investors. Kyle Quitman, the CEO, kept Marc as manager of the company he once owned. Marc was glad he could still work at his company and no longer had the stress of trying to find funding for his startup tech company.

Ravyn sent Marc to her office to collect her files and in mid-December set up to work from home. She found she could do a lot of phone calls from her bed, lying on her left side, but emails and editing stories from the freelancers took longer than she wanted.

By mid-January, she had to go ahead and take early maternity leave. She couldn't keep up with the work she needed to do.

As Harper's due date neared, Ravyn found herself depressed as well as uncomfortable.

"Jane, I'm miserable," she whined to her sister. "How did you stand the end of your pregnancy?"

Ravyn's sister Jane had given birth to her son Connor Nicholas Kennedy a few days before Christmas.

"Ravyn, it will all be worth it once you are holding your daughter in your arms. What did the doctor say the last time you saw her?"

"That if I am not in labor by next week, they are going to induce me. This baby girl better get her act together and get here."

"How is Marc doing?"

"He's still working. Why does he get his life and I don't get mine?" Ravyn whined.

"Ravyn, you are going to be a mother and your hormones are out of control. Your daughter will be here soon. Then you'll have other problems, like midnight feedings. Then you can be mad at Marc for not having boobs to nurse her."

Ravyn couldn't help herself, she burst out laughing. "Don't make me laugh. I'll pee myself!"

"Oh, and news flash, that may happen long after the baby comes."

"Oh no!"

"Oh yes. I had to wear maxi pads for a while after the birth. Hopefully, your girl won't be late. And have Marc help out."

"Help out?"

"You know, help out. Sex can be a way to jump-start labor."

"Oh, we've tried. Harper is just stubbornly snuggled in my womb."

"Well, OK. Have you tried eating spicy food?"

"That just gives me ferocious heartburn. We even got takeout from this place in Atlanta that swears by its eggplant Parmesan for making women go into labor."

"Well, just hang in there. We love you."

"Love you, too. Give Connor and Nick a kiss for me."

"Will do!"

Jane and Nick Kennedy had married in Greenville, South Carolina, at an outdoor park. It was a beautiful ceremony, Ravyn remembered. She'd stood up for her sister and had asked Jane to do the same for her at Ravyn's July wedding last year.

By that time both Jane and Ravyn were pregnant with their first children.

Ravyn rolled over onto her back. Her left hip was starting to ache. She'd had sciatica bad in that leg while pregnant and now that she was near her due date it seemed worse.

Ravyn rubbed her very pregnant belly. "Come on, baby girl. We want to meet you. Come on!"

Marc worked late at his office in Midtown Atlanta. He was trying to wrap up his work by Ravyn's due date, so he could stay home in anticipation of the birth.

For Valentine's Day, since the couple couldn't go out for dinner, Marc had opted for takeout at The Atlanta Fish Market, a seafood restaurant in Atlanta's Buckhead district, where Marc had proposed the previous year.

It was the final year as a couple without children. Marc had also picked up some roses from Publix. Ravyn had beamed at the gesture.

Marc smiled as he thought about becoming a father. And a father to a girl! He was especially excited about that as well. He hoped his newborn daughter looked just like her mother.

Marc could feel tears begin to well in his eyes and he quickly cleared his throat. No need to get all emotional, he told himself.

Marc was hoping he'd have time to go to the gym before he headed home. He liked the boxing class he had been taking and sparred with a couple of the trainers.

His favorite trainer was Joseph, a stocky Black man who pulled no punches. Marc had gone home with a bruised mouth after one recent session with Joseph. Ravyn had not been pleased.

It meant Marc hadn't been able to kiss Ravyn for a couple of days. But Ravyn hadn't forbidden Marc from continuing with his sport. Marc was trying to take it a bit easy at the gym as the birth of his daughter got closer. Just another day until Ravyn's due date. No need for him to risk an injury.

Marc looked at his watch and saw it was after 7 p.m. He'd better go, he thought. And he wouldn't have time to go to the gym. He texted Ravyn he was on his way home. He'd pick up something for dinner on the way home.

Marc stopped at a restaurant in Colony Square and got a takeout order. He then headed north on Peachtree into unusually heavy Atlanta traffic.

He got barely two blocks, just north of the High Museum, when he came to a dead stop. He couldn't see what the problem was, but all lanes, both northbound and southbound were jammed with traffic. He just knew he wasn't moving and couldn't get over into another lane to try a different route home.

Marc texted Ravyn he was stuck in traffic and hoped he'd be home soon.

Ravyn got Marc's text and sighed. She was hungry. She decided to get up and make a piece of toast. Maybe that would tide her over.

Ravyn got up and waddled into the kitchen. She reached up into the pantry and took out the bread. She dropped two slices in the toaster and got the peanut butter, too.

When the toast popped up, she put the peanut butter on and sat at the small bistro table and ate.

As she reached back up in the pantry to return the bread, Ravyn felt a bit of dampness in her underwear. Oh my God! I've wet myself again! she thought.

She waddled to the bathroom and tried to see how badly she'd wet herself. It was happening the closer she got to her due date. Ravyn reached down to try to remove her underwear and felt a stabbing back pain. Ravyn reached for her back to try to rub it and felt the pain ease.

Ravyn wrinkled her brow. Is this labor? Has my water broken?

Ravyn eased herself down on the toilet as she got her underwear down. She couldn't tell if it was pee or her water breaking. She got a new pair of underwear and put a pantiliner in her underwear.

She had to sit back down on the toilet to pull her underwear back up. Nothing was easy pregnant.

She got back into her bed and tried to relax. Marc would be home soon.

Ravyn started to doze off but was awakened by another pain in her back. Where was Marc? she wondered.

She reached over to get her iPhone to text Marc. Where are you?

Still stuck in traffic. I'm trying to get on a side street but it's gridlock. I've never seen it like this.

Accident?

I guess.

I'm not feeling well.

What's wrong?

I'm having back pain. It comes and goes.

Are you in labor?

I don't know. Hurry home.

I'll get there as soon as I can. I have takeout in the car. It will be cold by the time I get home.

Why don't you go ahead and eat it?

I don't want to eat without you.

I had some peanut butter toast. Go ahead and eat.

Love you.

Love you too.

Ravyn put her phone back on the nightstand and immediately felt a pain in her back. Maybe I should call the doctor, she thought.

Ravyn got the on-call nurse and told her about her back pain.

The nurse asked more questions and told Ravyn to begin timing the back pain. She was likely in labor. The nurse told Ravyn to call back in an hour. If the contractions were between five and ten minutes apart, she should go to Piedmont Hospital.

Ravyn tried not to panic. She began timing her contractions, but they were about 30 minutes apart.

She then called Marc.

"I'm in labor."

"You are? Dammit, I am still stuck in traffic. Can you get a taxi? I'll meet you at the hospital."

"The contractions aren't close enough yet to call a taxi. But I'm scared. Come home."

"Honey, I'm trying. What about a neighbor? Can Eleanor or Arthur take you?"

"I'll call over there, but I haven't seen either of their cars all day. I don't know that they are home."

"What about Julie?"

"I'll call her, but I think she was busy tonight. I tried to call her earlier and got her voicemail,"

"Oh no. Well, if all else fails, and only if there's no one else, call my brother Bruce. See if he can get there and be with you."

"Let me see if I can reach him."

"Seriously, only if there's no one else. I'm not sure you can count on him."

"Does he have a car?"

"My mother got him an old beater, so he does have a car now."

"That was nice of your mother."

"Made my father furious. He's threatened to cut Bruce out of his will."

"Would he do that?"

"Yes, he would," Marc said, anger in his voice. "I wouldn't be surprised if I'm out of his will, too."

"Oh, Marc, you are exaggerating."

"Sweetheart, I'm glad you think so, but my father would do it just for spite." Marc practically spat the word "spite" out.

"Well, I'll call your brother if I can't reach Eleanor or Julie."

"OK. Call me back when you know what you're doing. Love you."

"Love you, too."

Ravyn felt another contraction wave come over her. She bent over on the bed and tried to breathe through it. The contractions were coming closer. She tried not to panic and called her neighbor Eleanor, trying to keep her voice light when she got her voicemail.

"Hi Eleanor, it's Ravyn. I was hoping you were home tonight. I've gone into labor and Marc is stuck in horrible Atlanta traffic. I was hoping you could run me over to Piedmont Hospital. I'll call my friend or brother-in-law and see if they can bring me. Talk to you soon."

As Ravyn hung up, she realized how ridiculous her message sounded. Eleanor would probably panic when she got that message and rush over. If Ravyn reached Julie or Bruce, she'd call Eleanor back to let her know she had a ride.

Then she tried Julie.

Julie Montgomery was Ravyn's best friend in Atlanta. They'd been coworkers when they both worked for the daily newspaper. Julie left to get married and have children. Ravyn left when she was laid off during the Great Recession.

Ravyn got Julie's voicemail as well.

"Hi Jules. It's Ravyn. I'm in labor and Marc is stuck in some sort of major traffic jam in Atlanta. He's trying to get home but can't even get off on the side roads. I was hoping you were home and could take me to the hospital. Call back when you can."

Ravyn hung up and began to cry. She was scared.

Ravyn dried her tears and called Bruce next, getting his voicemail.

"Hi Bruce, this is Ravyn. I've gone into labor and need a ride to the hospital. I really don't want to call an ambulance or a taxi. Marc is stuck in some sort of epic traffic jam in Atlanta, but he says he'll meet me at the hospital if I can get there. Please call me back."

Ravyn hung up and tried to breathe calmly. Bruce would call her back. Bruce would come to get her if he could.

If he couldn't come or didn't call back, she needed to figure out how to get to the hospital.

Ravyn picked her phone up, then hung up and began to cry again.

Chapter 2

Ravyn stopped crying when her next contraction began. They were now about 15 minutes apart. She suddenly heard someone pounding on her front door. She got out of bed and waddled into the living room. It was dark out, but she could see a figure at her front door.

Oh, thank God! It must be Julie or Eleanor! Ravyn thought. She turned on her porch light.

She opened the door to see a panicked Bruce at the door.

"Bruce!"

"I got here as fast as I could," he said. "Let's go!"

"I need to grab my hospital bag."

"I'll get it. Where is it?"

"In my bedroom."

Bruce charged into the house, turned to see which bedroom was the master, and came back to the front door with the wrong bag.

"No, it's an overnight bag. It's a small suitcase. Pink with black polka dots."

"Oh."

He went back into the bedroom and came out to see Ravyn bent over with another contraction.

"Oh God, Ravyn! Are you OK?"

Ravyn was breathing, but unable to answer until the contraction ended. "I'm in labor," she panted. "I'm having contractions."

Bruce went to his car, put the bag in the trunk, then reached through the open passenger window and pulled the door handle through the window. He then yanked the passenger door open.

Ravyn carefully took the steps down the front porch one at a time. Bruce realized he needed to help her and rushed over to grab her arm to help her into the car.

Baby Steps

Ravyn looked down at the cloth passenger seat of Bruce's car. It was covered in dog fur.

"Um, do you have a towel for me to sit on?" she asked.

"Sorry, Blaze likes to ride in the car with me," he said. Blaze was Bruce's former stray dog. He'd adopted it after Marc and Ravyn's wedding, where Blaze created a small fire that set the wedding tent on fire.

Bruce reached down and tried to brush some of Blaze's fur off with his hand, but it only made the fur lift off the seat and swirl around before settling back on it.

"OK, forget it," Ravyn said. She realized she'd arrive at the hospital covered in dog fur.

Bruce helped Ravyn into the passenger seat, but her knees were crammed up against the dashboard in the car. "How can I push the seat back?"

"Umm, I don't know. Let me see if I can do it."

Bruce bent down and fumbled under Ravyn's legs to find the lever to push the passenger seat back. He pulled a lever and Ravyn's seat fell back. She was laying down, looking up at the ripped headliner.

"Ah!" She cried out. "My back!"

"Oh, sorry. That's not it."

With great effort, Bruce lifted the seat upright and began fumbling under the seat again.

Ravyn cried out with her next contraction.

"Bruce, forget it! Just drive!"

Bruce helped Ravyn with the seatbelt, reaching over her very large abdomen to snap it on. He was trying to move off her when his hand landed on her breast.

"Oh! Sorry, sorry! I didn't mean to touch you. Please don't tell Marc."

"Bruce, it was an accident. Please, can we just go? I'm scared."

"It was an accident. An accident. Really."

He ran around to the driver's side but was flustered as he started the car. He backed out and hit the mailbox at the end of the short driveway. Ravyn heard the crack of the wood and clang of the metal box hitting the roadway.

"Oh shit! What did I hit?"

"The mailbox. Just go!" Ravyn said, feeling another contraction coming. They were much closer together and she knew she should have already been at the hospital.

Bruce started down the street and sailed through a stop sign at the intersection, taking a hard left.

Ravyn yelped in surprise. "Bruce! The stop sign!"

"What stop sign?"

"The one you just ran! Please be careful. I want to get to the hospital in one piece."

As they barreled down the street, going much faster than the 35-mph speed limit, Ravyn saw Julie's car speeding toward her house. "Julie!"

"What?" Bruce asked.

Ravyn tried to turn around in the seat, but she couldn't. "That was my friend, Julie. Going toward my house."

"Should I turn around and go back?"

Ravyn's reply came with a groan of pain. "Keep driving," she cried.

Ravyn slowly got her cellphone out of her handbag and called Julie.

"Ravyn! Where are you? I'm at your house and you aren't answering your door. And your mailbox is in the street."

"You passed us. Bruce is taking me to the hospital. He hit the mailbox by accident. Please come to the hospital."

"Bruce?"

"Please hurry. I'm scared."

"OK. I'm on my way there. Piedmont right?"

"Yes."

"Did you call your doctor?"

"I'll do that now."

"Which way now?" Bruce asked, when he came to the intersection with Peachtree Road.

"Turn left. It's not far, maybe a couple of miles. When you get to get to the top of the hill you'll see the Shepherd Center, you'll turn right at the light."

Bruce nodded, gripping the steering wheel so hard Ravyn could see his knuckles go white. Ravyn called her doctor letting her know she was on the way and telling her the contractions were about five minutes apart.

Bruce didn't speak until they were passing the Shepherd Center. "I turn right here, right?"

"At the light."

Bruce stopped the car, waiting for traffic, but the light turned yellow, then red. "Now what?"

"Just wait for the light. You'll get the green soon."

Bruce began to tap the steering wheel impatiently.

"Bruce, it will be OK."

"I just don't want to mess up. I really like you."

Ravyn was touched, but another contraction began. Maybe they were less than the five minutes apart she'd told her doctor. She hadn't really been keeping track. She was too nervous. But they were only a left turn and a right turn away from the hospital entrance.

"Bruce, I think you should drop me off at the emergency room. Then park the car and come in and find me. And call Marc and tell him we are here."

Bruce nodded, his eyes wide with fright. "You'll be OK, right?"

"It will be fine. I'm just having a baby."

"OK."

Julie's car was right behind Bruce, beeping the horn when the light turned green. Bruce turned and Julie turned right behind him.

Bruce pulled up to the emergency entrance and Julie parked behind him. Julie got out and ran into the entrance, flagging down a nurse.

A nurse quickly came out with a wheelchair for Ravyn.

Bruce helped Ravyn out of the car and Bruce and the nurse got her into the wheelchair. As she was wheeled into the emergency room entrance, Ravyn called out, "Thanks, Bruce! Call Marc! And bring my bag!"

Julie and Bruce entered Ravyn's birthing suite. Ravyn had changed into a hospital gown and tried to cover her knees when they both came in. A fetal monitor was strapped across Ravyn's belly.

"Any word on Marc?" she asked anxiously.

"He's coming," Bruce said, averting his eyes away from Ravyn. "He said there was a bad wreck on Peachtree, blocking all lanes. But he's coming."

"Did he say when he would get here? My contractions are close. He's my birthing coach," Ravyn said, suddenly her lower lip began to quiver, and she burst into tears.

"Oh, Ravyn, he will be here. You know he's frantically trying to get here," Julie said, coming beside Ravyn's hospital bed and giving her hand a squeeze. "How far apart are your contractions?"

"Ten minutes. I thought they were closer together. They felt closer together."

"You've still got some time. So, Marc still has time to get here."

"What if my baby gets here before he does?"

"I'll be your coach if he's not here," Julie said. "I've given birth twice and my husband was not all that helpful, even though we went through the classes twice."

"Will you? Will you be my coach if he's not here?"

"Of course, I will."

Dr. Brenda Watkins, the OB/GYN came into the room and told Ravyn she was progressing, but it might be a while. She asked if Ravyn wanted an epidural.

"I'm not sure," Ravyn said, at the same time Julie said, "Yes."

"Yes?" Ravyn asked. "Marc and I talked about trying natural childbirth."

"Oh honey, that's because he's not birthing a watermelon out of his penis. You want an epidural. You do not want to feel everything. Trust me."

Bruce turned pale at Julie's comment. Ravyn looked at her OB/GYN unsure.

"What do you say?" she asked her doctor.

"Ravyn, this is your choice."

"Did you have an epidural?"

Dr. Watkins shook her head in the affirmative.

"OK. I want an epidural."

"Coming right up," the doctor said and left the room to find an anesthesiologist to administer the epidural.

Ravyn felt another contraction begin and wailed in pain. Julie took hold of Ravyn's hand again. "Breathe, Ravyn. Breathe evenly."

"I don't feel so good," Bruce said, sitting down in a nearby chair.

"You don't look so good," Julie said, turning to look at him. "Do you feel faint?"

Bruce could only shake his head.

"Put your head between your knees," Julie commanded. "Are you going to be sick?"

Bruce put his head down and shook his head.

Julie let go of Ravyn's hand and quickly grabbed a nearby waste can. She put it under Bruce's head just as he was sick.

Julie rubbed Bruce's back until he stopped vomiting. "Nurse!" Julie called out.

A nurse hustled in, asking, "Is this the father? Usually, this happens when they see all the blood."

At the word blood, Bruce became sick again.

"That's not the father," Ravyn assured. "Bruce is my brother-in-law. My husband is still on his way here."

"OK, let's get you out of the room," the nurse said to Bruce. "Let's get your blood pressure and see what's going on."

Bruce looked up, afraid. "I don't want to leave Ravyn," he whispered.

"Honey, you got her here safely," Julie said in a soothing voice. "Your job is done here. Let the nurse help you. Maybe get a cold compress on your head and neck. You will feel better soon."

"What if Marc comes and I'm not here? He'll think I didn't help."

"Ravyn and I will both tell him you were here and helped tremendously. Bruce, you need to take care of yourself now. Especially if you aren't feeling well."

Bruce nodded and the nurse brought around a wheelchair and helped him in it. Bruce gave a small wave as he was wheeled out of the birthing suite.

"Is he going to be OK?" Ravyn asked.

"I'm sure he was just overwhelmed with what is happening right now," Julie said.

Ravyn felt her next contraction begin and tried to control her breathing but found herself hyperventilating. Julie quickly handed her a paper bag on the nightstand and gave it to Ravyn, who began to breathe into it.

The epidural was administered. Ravyn didn't realize how bad it would hurt. She started to cry.

Julie held her hand through the process.

Ravyn's doctor re-entered the room and checked Ravyn. She was close to being fully dilated. Then Dr. Watkins looked at Julie. "Are you going to be here for the birth?"

"Ravyn's husband was in really bad traffic. There was an accident blocking Peachtree. He's trying to get here. I'll stand in until he gets here."

"I need you to scrub up and gown up then," Dr. Watkins said.

Julie did as she was told, scrubbing her hands, and allowing the nurse to help her put on a gown and hair cap.

Ravyn began to cry again. "I want Marc," she wailed.

"Honey, he's coming. I'll just be here until he comes. You know he's probably jogging up Peachtree to try to get here."

Ravyn snorted a laugh through her tears. "He can't run."

"Well, he's walking briskly then."

Ravyn smiled through her tears.

Julie was talking Ravyn through the birth, getting her to push when needed, but the baby's head wasn't crowning. The doctor said she'd have to perform an episiotomy and Julie inwardly cringed.

As the doctor was making the necessary cuts to Ravyn's vagina, Marc ran into the room. "I'm here! I'm here!" he said out of breath. "I can help!"

Julie saw the relief on Ravyn's face and stepped away. The doctor and nurse both told Marc to scrub up and put on a gown, which he did.

Two hours after his arrival, Marc was cutting the umbilical cord of his newborn daughter.

Marc could not stop his tears as he placed Harper Shaw Linder on Ravyn's chest.

Marc returned to the master bedroom with Harper in his arms. "Sorry, Ravyn. I changed her, but I think she wants you."

Ravyn yawned, stretched her arms, and held them out for Harper. Marc placed their daughter in her arms. Ravyn cradled Harper, then unbuttoned her nightgown and gave Harper her breast. Harper began to suck greedily.

Ravyn softly stroked Harper's cheek as her daughter looked up at her. Ravyn's heart melted every time she looked into her daughter's eyes.

Marc put his hand on Ravyn's shoulder. "You are a beautiful mother, Ravyn."

Ravyn looked up at him and beamed. "I didn't know I could be this happy."

Marc leaned down and kissed Ravyn, then cupped his daughter's head. "She's beautiful, just like her mother."

"I think she's got your mouth."

"Thankfully she's got your cute nose and beautiful blue eyes."

"Marc, most baby's eyes are blue at birth. They change as they get older. Maybe she'll have your beautiful hazel eyes."

"I hope she gets your blue eyes. I hope they don't change. Hey, I've got to head into the office today. I won't be long. I'll be home by lunch. Will you two be alright without me?"

"We will be fine. I'm going to hate going back to work next week. I hated being on early maternity leave. I feel like I got cheated being on bed rest. Now that she's here, I just want to stay home with her."

"If you want to stay home, why don't you quit your job?"

"Marc, we need my income. Besides, I don't want to. I like what I do. I get fulfillment being an editor at the magazine. Plus, I want our daughter to see a strong working mother."

"OK, so don't quit your job. Harper can start daycare at Colony Square. She'll be six weeks by the time she goes."

"Thank God you thought to get her into that Montessori program. I would have been scrambling to find something."

"Hey, I'm good at some things."

"Getting our daughter into a good daycare makes me love you even more," Ravyn said.

Marc kissed Ravyn then bent down to kiss his daughter's head before heading into the shower.

Two weeks after Harper began daycare and Ravyn returned to work, Ravyn got home to find a package at her doorstep. It wasn't that she was surprised by packages. Baby gifts were coming to the house almost every day.

Kyle Quitman had sent a case of wine from Star 1 Winery. Ravyn knew she'd be able to enjoy the wine in a few months and she and Marc had stored it in the guest bedroom.

What did surprise her when she opened this gift was it was from Laura Lucas. Inside there was a bathroom scale and a book on how to keep yourself fit after a baby. Ravyn burst into tears.

Baby Steps

When she'd pulled herself together, Ravyn called Marc. Now furious with Laura, Ravyn told Marc what she'd sent.

"She's just evil, Marc! Why be such a cruel person? I hate her. I just hate her," Ravyn exclaimed.

"That's a really rotten thing to send you, but you should see what she sent me."

"What did she send you? Did she send it to your office?"

"She did. But maybe I shouldn't tell you. It might upset you more," Marc said, thinking about Laura's gift to him.

"No, tell me. I want to know."

"She sent me a DNA test kit."

"What?" Ravyn screeched. "Is she implying that Harper isn't yours? I want to tear her eyes out. I better never see that bitch again or you'll have to bail me out of jail."

"I threw the test away. It's in the garbage because that gift is garbage. I'm sure she sent it just to be cruel to both of us."

"Well, she sure knows how to be hateful. Just hateful. I don't know what you ever saw in her."

"I certainly didn't see a woman I wanted to spend the rest of my life with," Marc said, trying to soothe Ravyn. "Listen, throw those items out. And why don't you pump some milk tonight so we can break out one of those bottles of Star 1 wine. You and I will need to unwind from Laura's not-so-subtle gifts."

"That sounds like a great idea. Hurry home so we can enjoy the wine."

"I should probably pick up some steaks. That would be great with that Cabernet Kyle sent."

"That sounds fabulous. I'm glad it's Friday. I don't want to enjoy the wine too much and make both of us late for work tomorrow."

"Darling, our daughter will never let us sleep in or be late for work again."

Ravyn could only laugh. Her husband was right.

Ravyn had learned the secret of all moms everywhere. When Harper went down for a nap on the weekends, so did Ravyn. At first, Ravyn tried to get housework done when Harper napped, but then she realized she was just more exhausted when Harper woke up.

Her cracked nipples had finally healed months ago, and she could finally nurse Harper without wincing. And she'd only had one freak out with the brown flecks in her daughter's diaper before she called her pediatrician. All normal, he said.

Ravyn's cellphone rang shortly after Harper woke up from her mid-morning nap and Ravyn was excited to see it was Julie.

"Jules! How are you?"

"Good. Are you ready to get out of the house?"

"Oh my God, I am! What do you want to do?"

"Let's have lunch. My treat. And bring your adorable daughter. I want to just sniff that baby smell."

"You know I'm not leaving her behind. Where and when?"

"Let's go to this new place I found in Brookhaven. Olde Blind Dog. It's an Irish bar. They seriously have one of the best Rueben sandwiches I've ever eaten."

"Sounds good. What time?"

"Let's say around noon. Is that OK? Is Marc home today?"

"Believe it or not, he's at work."

"On a Saturday?"

"He's got a new project and he's been putting in some extra hours. I'll text him. He'll probably be relieved because with us out of the house, he can go to the gym when he leaves his office."

"Great. I'll see you soon."

"Thanks, Julie."

"I'm not doing it for you. I want to see Harper!"

Ravyn pulled into the parking lot near the restaurant in Town Brookhaven. She still wasn't used to driving her new SUV. They had traded in her Honda Civic for a new 2016 Honda CR-V shortly after she realized it was difficult to get in and out of the car with her pregnant belly.

Although the new car was easier to get in and out of – and was needed for the baby seat and stuff she now needed to carry around – Ravyn still cried when she left her blue Honda Civic, she'd named Sapphire on the trade-in lot.

She consoled herself with a darker blue color: Obsidian Blue Pearl. So, it was like a darker shade of sapphire, she reasoned. She also liked the leather heated seats. When her back ached she often wanted to go sit in her car.

Ravyn was so used to driving a smaller car. Despite the backup camera in her new car, she'd already nearly wiped out the replacement mailbox at the end of the driveway. The one Bruce had nailed when she had gone into labor that February 17. Harper was born in the early morning hours of February 18.

Ravyn got Harper out of her car seat and grabbed the large Kate Spade diaper bag Jane had given her as a baby shower gift.

Ravyn had never had a Kate Spade handbag in her life and now the diaper bag for her daughter was nicer and more expensive than her own Macy's handbag.

Ravyn entered the dimly lit restaurant and was happy to see Julie standing just inside waiting for her. They were led to a table near the back and Ravyn put Harper's car carrier on the table until the server brought over a high chair.

Ravyn then strapped Harper in the high chair and put the car carrier on the chair next to her.

"I really like your diaper bag. Super cute. My God, they never had something so cute when my girls were little," Julie exclaimed.

"My mother said the same thing," she replied.

Julie laughed. "Well, things only improve when it comes to baby gear. Are you and Marc getting much sleep, or does Harper keep you up at night?"

"My husband could sleep through a freight train plowing into the house. I, on the other hand, hear every time she rolls over and sighs. She is mostly sleeping through the night, but if I hear a peep on the baby monitor, I'm up and at her crib. Then it takes me a while to get back to sleep. I apologize if I look like a raccoon today."

"Are you still pumping some extra milk?"

"I am but I'm starting her on solid food. Still, I keep a couple of extra bottles in the fridge. That way Marc can get up to feed her in the middle of the night if she wakes up. And it means I can have a glass of wine at night if I need it."

"Smart woman."

Julie and Ravyn ordered their lunches and Ravyn wiped down the table in front of Harper, laying down some toasted oat cereal in front of her high chair.

"She's getting so big!" Julie exclaimed. "I can't believe she'll be seven months old."

"Next week. I know you told me time and again to live every moment because it goes by so quickly. And it has. I'm going to be a crying mess when she's ready for kindergarten."

Harper gladly picked up the toasted cereal and put it in her mouth. Or tried to. Not each one made it. Several found their way onto the floor.

"Maybe we should have eaten outside," Ravyn said. "Harper is going to make a mess."

"I am quite certain you are not the first mother with an infant who has made a mess of their floor. We will just tip well."

Ravyn laughed.

When their meals arrived, Ravyn asked Julie, "Can I ask you a personal question about sex after giving birth?"

"That it is uncomfortable after that episiotomy or that your vajajay isn't quite as tight anymore and you have a hard time orgasming?"

"Ok, you kind of answered two of my questions. But did Rob kind of not want to make love after the birth of your girls?"

"Is Marc ignoring you?"

"Not really. We tried to make love several weeks after the birth, and it was so painful for me. We haven't really tried again. We even missed having sex on our anniversary!"

"What? That's criminal."

"It wasn't planned. Harper picked up some stomach bug at daycare, then I got it. I slept in the guest room so Marc wouldn't get sick too."

"If he loves you, he should be willing to get sick by having mad passionate sex with you," Julie said.

Ravyn rolled her eyes at her friend.

"So really, nothing between you two?"

"I mean, I give him blow jobs, but nothing in my area."

"He doesn't go down on you?"

"He does, but there's been no sex sex. And I'm exhausted at night so it might be my fault. Is this normal?"

"Honey, you are both new parents, and being new parents is exhausting. He'll be in the mood, and you aren't, or you're in the mood and he isn't. It's like you both got out of sync."

"Exactly!"

"I know it sounds kind of clinical, but you might have to schedule when you have sex. And it might not be at night. It could be as soon as Harper goes down for a nap."

"That's when I nap," Ravyn smiled.

"Well, tomorrow you two have sex when she naps."

"OK. Thanks for telling me I'm normal."

"You most certainly are normal. Now my husband is another matter."

"What do you mean?"

"I can count the number of times we've made love since my surgery, and I can't use two hands."

"Really? I'm so sorry. Is it Rob? Does he need, ah, help?"

"You mean Viagra? I suggested it and he got defensive and mad. All that lubricant we bought at the sexy shop is going to waste," Julie said, a tear rolling down her cheek. She quickly wiped it away and tried to smile.

Ravyn reached over and put her hand on Julie's and gave it a squeeze.

Harper began to get fussy and Ravyn reached into her baby bag for some baby food and spoon. Harper leaned in when the spoon got near her mouth.

"She's a good little eater," Julie said. "Lexie was such a fussy eater. She'd have food all over her face, the high chair, her hair. Now Ashley was my good eater," she said of her two daughters.

"Oh, Harper can be squirmy and want to play with her food. There are times I just take her into the shower with me to clean her."

Baby Steps

"Yep. The shower hand-off. You and Marc are going to be old pros when your next one comes."

"Don't jinx me! I want to wait at least two years, maybe three. I'd like Harper to be potty trained before I think of the next one."

As if on cue, Harper began to grab for the spoon and turn her face as Ravyn tried to feed her more baby food.

"I guess my little darling is done," she said, capping the jar of baby food and pulling out a baby wipe to clean Harper, but Harper squirmed to keep Ravyn from cleaning her face and hands. Ravyn then put everything back in her bag.

When they were nearly finished with their lunches, Harper made a face and let out a giant fart.

"Oh, sorry. She's been a little gassy the last couple of days."

Ravyn looked down and to her horror yellow diarrhea began to leak out of the leg holes of Harper's diaper. Ravyn's eyes got wide.

"What's wrong?" Julie asked.

"Explosive diarrhea!"

Ravyn quickly got Harper out of the high chair and ran with her daughter to the women's restroom. She took off Harper's cute little matching shirt and skirt and threw those in the sink, running water over the outfit. She then used an entire box of baby wipes to wipe her daughter down from head to foot.

How the hell had she gotten poo in her hair? Ravyn wondered. It was like the poo had traveled up her daughter's back.

Harper began to cry as Ravyn laid her head gently under the faucet and used the restaurant soap to try to wash her hair. Ravyn then put baby lotion on her as best she could since Harper was now squirming to get out of Ravyn's grasp.

Ravyn dressed Harper in a new outfit and strapped Harper to the baby changing station to see what she should do about the soiled outfit. It was so cute, and a gift from her co-worker Kristine, but she wasn't sure it was worth trying to save.

With a sigh, she wrapped the stained and smelly outfit in a plastic bag she kept in her baby bag and buried it deep in the restroom trash.

When Ravyn returned to the table, she could see a busboy cleaning up the puddles of diarrhea under the high chair. Ravyn began to cry. "I'm out of wipes!"

"It's OK, Ravyn. This young man will get it up."

"I'm so sorry," Ravyn said to the young man.

The young waitress came over with a wrinkled nose and put the check on the table. Julie put her credit card down and the waitress took it immediately.

"She's giving us the stink eye, but just wait until she has kids one day," Julie said.

Ravyn tried to smile, but the events after lunch had turned into a disaster. Julie left a more than generous tip and she and Ravyn went to their cars.

"I'm never going to be able to come back here again," Ravyn lamented.

"We'll just come back when Harper is 18."

Ravyn gave Julie a crooked smile.

Chapter 3

Ravyn got home to find Marc gone. She unloaded Harper and the baby bag and headed into the house. She planned to get in the shower with her daughter, but Harper had fallen asleep in the car, so she'd put her down in her crib to see if she'd still sleep.

Harper cried just a few sobs, then went back into dreamland.

Ravyn was wiped out. She laid on the couch and fell asleep, awaking when she heard the lock on the front door open.

"Oh, hey, I didn't mean to wake you," Marc said, entering the home and coming over to kiss Ravyn.

"It was kind of a crazy lunch. Harper had a huge diaper blowout. Poop was all over her, her hair, her cute outfit. I had to throw the outfit out. It was ruined."

Marc made a face. "That sounds appetizing."

"Thankfully she did it after we finished eating."

"Where is she now?"

"She fell asleep in the car, so I put her down in her crib and she kept sleeping. Then I came in to lie on the couch and I fell asleep too. Guess we were both tired after our afternoon out. Did you go to the gym?"

"Yes, and I need to shower."

"I wish Harper was up, you could take her in with you and scrub her down. I could only clean her up with baby wipes in the restroom."

"Do you want me to wake her?"

"Not really. If she's got a tummy bug, she may just want to sleep."

"OK. I won't be long," he said, heading into the master bedroom. A few minutes later, Ravyn could hear the shower running.

Ravyn got up and went to Harper's crib. She was still sleeping, but Ravyn felt her cheek to see if she was running a fever. Her cheeks looked pink.

Ravyn got the ear thermometer and gently put it in Harper's ear. She had a temperature of 100 degrees. Ravyn knew it would be a long night of checking on Harper every hour. Ravyn sighed. So much for trying to make love to her husband tonight.

At five o'clock the next morning, Ravyn fell into her marital bed exhausted. Harper's fever had broken. She and Marc had taken turns throughout the night to check on her.

Marc stirred and put his arm over his wife. "Is Harper OK?"

"The fever's broken. She's asleep. I am so tired."

"Maybe we can sleep in a little," he said.

"God, I hope so. I gave her a little children's pain reliever, so I hope she'll sleep a little longer. We both need some sleep," Ravyn said, but she could hear Marc beginning his soft snore.

Ravyn envied that he could sleep so easily and quickly. She laid awake for another hour before she finally fell asleep. But she awoke with a start an hour later to Harper's cries.

Mark opened his eyes. "I'll get her. You sleep."

"I love you," Ravyn said, sleepily.

Marc lifted Harper out of her crib, changed her diaper, and padded into the kitchen to get her baby food. He picked a jar of banana, mango, and sweet potatoes. "I hope you like this," he said to his daughter. "I'd rather have eggs, bacon, and orange juice. We'll get you some of that when you are a little older."

Marc got Harper in her high chair, put on a little bib that read "Daddy's Best Girl" and fed his daughter. He did the airplane motion and made the noises, which made Harper laugh and clap her hands before she opened her mouth for the food.

"Here comes the airplane," he said, swirling the spoon toward Harper. "Open the gate!"

Marc made a noise like an engine. Harper grinned and pounded on the high chair, opening her mouth when the spoon got close.

After a few minutes, Marc realized Ravyn was standing at the kitchen door, smiling.

"Oh, I thought you were going to sleep in. I've got it here."

"I know you do. You are a natural father to our daughter," she said, walking over to hug her husband from behind.

"Hey, you are interrupting the flight plans at Hartsfield," Marc kidded. "We can't have our daughter waiting at the gate."

"How about I get our breakfast? Eggs, bacon, and coffee?"

"And orange juice."

"And orange juice."

"You know me so well. I told Harper what's ahead for her and breakfast when she's a little older," he said, looking at the baby food label. "I'm not so sure about bananas, mango, and sweet potatoes for breakfast."

Ravyn got the coffee pot started, making a full pot. Then she pulled out a dozen eggs and the bacon from the refrigerator. "Do you want your eggs scrambled, poached, or an omelet?"

"Do we have stuff for an omelet?"

"I think we've got ham and cheese, and I know we have onions. There may be some green peppers too."

"Sounds great. Let's do that."

Ravyn put the omelet pan on the gas stove and started the flame. She added a pat of butter and let it begin to sizzle before she cracked the eggs. Ravyn was proud she could make a decent omelet.

She put the bacon in the microwave. Marc liked it extra crispy. She turned on the fan to keep the smoke down.

Ravyn plated the omelets and bacon, poured the coffee and orange juice, and put it on the table. Marc had finished feeding Harper, who began to reject his airplane swooshing spoon.

Marc picked up his fork and began eating his omelet. "This is great. Thanks for fixing breakfast."

Ravyn and Marc chatted over breakfast while Harper entertained herself with a plastic set of keys, chewing on them, then banging them on the plastic tray of the high chair.

Marc reached over and grabbed Ravyn's left hand. "I love you."

"I love you too."

"Do you think Harper can entertain herself in her playpen for a little while?"

"Maybe."

"We could entertain ourselves elsewhere."

"I'd like that."

"I would too. I feel like it's been too long…"

"It has been too long."

Ravyn finished her last bite of breakfast and put the plates in the sink while Marc brought Harper to her playpen. He also brought her a bottle, just in case she wanted it, and would go to sleep.

With Harper in the playpen, Marc and Ravyn went back into the bedroom. They certainly entertained themselves and they fell asleep in each other's arms, spent from late morning sex and a sleeping, sated Harper.

Ravyn's alarm went off first that Monday morning, then Marc's. They both were still tired from taking turns to check on Harper all Saturday night. Even though they'd taken naps on Sunday, it was never enough.

Did all parents feel just sheer exhaustion the first year of their child's life? Ravyn wondered. Thank goodness she'd set the programmable coffee maker the night before. She thought she and Marc would need extra cups for today.

Ravyn felt like she and Marc were in a good routine with Harper. Ravyn gave Harper a quick breastfeed in the morning while Marc took his shower. She knew she'd be binding her breasts soon, but she did love the intimate moments with her daughter. She would miss it.

Then Ravyn jumped into the shower to get ready while Marc dressed Harper and got her ready for daycare. He packed her baby bag with extra diapers, her organic baby food, and an extra outfit — just in case.

Then Marc and Ravyn kissed at the door as Marc took Harper to the Colony Square Montessori school, while Ravyn headed to her job in downtown Atlanta.

At the end of Ravyn's day, she drove to Colony Square to pick up her daughter by six o'clock. Marc generally stayed later to work on his new project, then went to his gym and three times a week to his boxing class, before coming home.

Ravyn often fed Harper, then put her to bed around seven o'clock, then she and Marc had dinner together before Marc went in to kiss his daughter good night. Marc and Ravyn found themselves in bed by nine thirty, or no later than ten o'clock. And the next morning they started the routine all over again. It was a grinding week for each of them.

By the time they got to the weekend, they were both spent. They tried to take turns getting up with Harper in the morning, but sometimes she was up at five o'clock in the morning, and some weekend mornings she slept in until seven o'clock. Marc and Ravyn lived for those mornings when they both got to sleep in just a little bit longer.

Chapter 4

Julie called Ravyn in tears. Ravyn couldn't quite understand Julie through her sobs.

"What's wrong?" Ravyn pleaded. "Are the girls OK? Did something happen at their school?"

"It's Rob."

"What's wrong with Rob?"

"He wants a divorce."

"What?" Ravyn exclaimed, shocked. "Why?"

"He says he doesn't love me. He's been having an affair at work, with one of his co-workers."

Ravyn was speechless, but in thinking back to the time last May when she stayed at Julie's house, caring for Julie's daughters Ashley and Lexie after Julie's oophorectomy surgery, which removed her ovaries, she remembered Rob was often at his office, not at home or at the hospital with Julie.

"Did he tell you he was having an affair?"

"He didn't have to. I found Viagra in his gym bag. Lord knows he wasn't using it on me," Julie said bitterly. "I confronted him, and he told me about the affair. I begged him to go back to counseling. He refused. Then he told me he wanted a divorce."

"Julie, I don't know what to say. Do you and the girls need somewhere to stay? We can put you up temporarily."

"We are at a hotel for now. I don't know what to do. Rob says he wants the house. I've called a divorce attorney, and she told me some preliminary things to put in place, but I just don't know what to do."

Julie began to cry and Ravyn felt her heartbreak for her friend. Inwardly, she cursed Rob and his wandering penis.

"I'm so sorry," was all Ravyn could say. Then Ravyn began to cry. It was all so unfair. She thought Julie and Rob had worked through their marital difficulties and his previous infidelity. Clearly, they hadn't. Or he hadn't. Now Rob wanted a divorce?

Marc came in, worried at hearing Ravyn crying. She looked up and mouthed "Julie." He took her hand, gave it a little squeeze, and left the living room.

"Where are you? At a hotel in Buckhead?" Ravyn asked.

"I wouldn't tell Rob where I was going. We're at a hotel in Midtown. Thank God I have my own credit card. He can't see where we are right now, and he didn't follow me. I told the girls to pack a bag and here we are."

"Are you safe?"

"I don't think Rob wants anything but the divorce, and the house."

"The house? Why does he want the house? Where will you live? Where would the girls go? Would they live with you or Rob?"

Julie said she would fight to get the majority custody of her daughters, but it also meant she was going to have to re-enter the workforce. What skills did she have now? She'd been a stay-at-home mother for over 10 years.

"I just don't know what will happen, Ravyn. I just don't know."

Ravyn said she could hire Julie for some freelance articles for *Cleopatra*, the lifestyle magazine where Ravyn worked, but it didn't pay all that much.

Julie said knew she was going to have to take some classes and find something full-time. It would kill her to not be there for her daughters after school.

"This is all Rob's fault!" Julie shouted into the phone. "I'm so angry with him. He's destroying our family."

"Where are you? You sound like you are in an echo chamber," Ravyn said.

"I'm in the bathroom. It was the only place with a little bit of privacy."

Ravyn could hear wailing in the background.

"Ravyn, I've got to go. Ashley is crying and Lexie is just rocking back and forth. She won't even talk. I'm worried about both of them. Can I just say how much I hate Rob?"

"Should you have them see a counselor?"

"Maybe. Probably. It's all so overwhelming. I'll talk to the school. Maybe they have someone they can talk to there. I can't be the first Buckhead mother to go through a divorce."

"I love you, Julie. I'll help you in any way I can."

"Thank you. Love you too."

"What was all that about?" Marc asked, concerned.

"Rob is divorcing Julie. He's cheating on her again."

"Oh my God. I'm sorry to hear that."

"You know what, I think he was cheating last year when I looked after the girls."

"How do you know?"

"I really don't, but his behavior was so odd. Julie was in the hospital recovering from her surgery and he would go to his office to work late. That's what he told me. He was probably meeting his co-worker."

"He cheated on Julie with a co-worker?"

"That's what Julie said."

"How did she find out?"

"She found Viagra in his gym bag and knew he wasn't using it on her."

"That's really bad."

"She's angry with him and I'm furious. She's such a good person. She doesn't deserve this."

"No, she doesn't. Is she at her house?"

"No. She took the girls and is staying at a hotel."

"She's at a hotel?"

"Yeah. He should have moved out. I'm hating him even more. Men can be such rat bastards."

"I'm not going to defend Rob, but this rat bastard loves you and our daughter very much," Marc said, kissing Ravyn on the top of her head.

"I didn't mean you were a rat bastard, just Rob," Ravyn said. "It's just so upsetting."

"If it's any consolation, I've always liked her more than him. He just... I never got a good feeling about him. And that whole mix-up when I sent Julie the flowers."

Marc had sent Julie roses for her helping him get back together with Ravyn and Julie's husband had hit the roof, accusing Julie of seeing someone. "In hindsight, maybe he was acting out at her because he was seeing someone."

"The pot calling the kettle black, right?"

"Right."

Marc and Ravyn both heard Harper starting to babble on the baby monitor.

"She's going to say her first word soon," Ravyn said. "I just hope she does it at home and not at the daycare center. I don't want strangers to hear my daughter's first words."

"I just bet she'll say mama first. Don't you think so?"

"She might say dada. Both sounds are easy to make. I just know whenever she does start talking, she'll have a lot to say."

Marc laughed. "Just like her mama."

Ravyn made a face at her husband but didn't disagree.

Over the next two weeks, Marc tried to do more chores, help get the groceries, and tend to Harper. He was going a little overboard to show he wasn't like Rob, and Ravyn appreciated it.

But slowly Marc went back to letting Ravyn do the lion's share of the housework, grocery shopping, and caring for Harper.

Ravyn began to feel neglected once again. She talked to Julie daily now, mostly listening to Julie complain about Rob and how he was intentionally trying to gaslight her.

"He keeps telling me I was the one who stopped loving him," Julie ranted. "That I became cold and distant. Hell no! He was the one who stopped loving me! He never even touched me after my surgery. That bastard."

Then Julie began to cry again. Ravyn was worried about Julie's mental health. Julie had gotten her daughters to see a counselor, but they just cried the whole time and begged their mother not to make them go back.

Julie got them to go to one more session but realized it was fruitless until they were ready to talk about what was happening and how it made them feel. Plus, she had to watch every cent these days and couldn't really afford the counselor's fee.

Julie's divorce attorney had said the best and easiest way for the divorce to go through was through mediation. Each side would hammer out the terms of the divorce and then it would go before a judge.

Julie had to go through the house and take photos of things that were hers: her furniture, her jewelry, her clothing. Julie told Ravyn that was the hardest part because much of the furniture she and Rob had bought as a couple.

Much of her jewelry was gifts Rob had given her over the years. Some of the jewelry she would put away to give to her daughters someday. Some she would likely have to sell after the divorce. Julie was very worried about her finances.

She told Ravyn she'd stopped wearing her engagement and wedding ring. She was wearing an opal ring she'd gotten before she'd gotten married. It just felt too strange to not have a ring on her left hand.

Ravyn listened with an empathetic ear. She made some suggestions where she could, but mostly she listened to her friend rant and grieve. Rob and Julie had been married for nearly 15 years and Ravyn knew this was a big loss for her friend.

"Listen, I want to take you out to lunch," Ravyn said. "How about this weekend? Can you get away? And this is my treat. You need it."

"Rob and I are spending every other weekend at an Airbnb, just so we don't have to be in the same house all weekend. He will not move out. Says it will be his house soon enough. Fucker. I hate him. I can't believe I was once in love with him. In about six weeks this will be over. I'm apartment hunting, but I'll make time for lunch."

"Great. What about Del Frisco Grill? It's right there at the Mandarin Oriental in Buckhead."

"Sounds lovely. Want to pick me up at my Airbnb on Sunday?"

"I'd love to. Will the girls be with you?"

"No, I told Rob he can keep the girls when I'm at the Airbnb so he can get used to taking care of them every other weekend. He did not like that. Because with the girls there, he can't bring his whore over to spend the night."

"And you get some much-needed time to yourself."

"Yes. I need time to think, to work out what my next steps are. I can't do that with the girls listening to my every word. They are being clingy, too. I know it's because of the divorce. I'm sure on his weekend at the Airbnb that whore is with him."

"What an ass."

"I agree. But I think it will work in my favor, his having to watch the girls on my weekend at the Airbnb."

"How so?"

"I honestly think he won't fight me for full custody. Probably not even 50/50. The girls tell me he practically ignores them the weekends they are with him. They have to remind him when it is lunch and dinner. Usually, he's ordering pizza."

"That's awful. Listen, I'll come to pick you up Sunday at about eleven o'clock. I'll make reservations for 11:30. How about that? That way we only have to valet my car."

"See you then."

Ravyn pulled up to a cute apartment in Midtown and called Julie's number. She came down to meet Ravyn in her car.

"Is your Airbnb cute?" Ravyn asked.

"They've all been nice. And I get to see some neighborhoods where I might want to rent," Julie said. "I just can't be too far away from Walden Academy. Rob has agreed they won't have to change schools. At least not for now."

"That's good news. Is he paying for it?" Ravyn asked, knowing Walden was a private prep school near Buckhead.

"He'll have to. I won't be making any money."

"I have some assignments I can give you if you're ready to take some freelance."

"Not sure I can take anything right now, with the divorce still pending. As soon as it's complete, I will want some freelance work from you. I am also job hunting. It's been rough. Being a woman of a certain age re-entering the job market is no fun. I'm competing against young women who will work crazy hours for no pay. I just can't do that."

"Will Rob pay alimony?"

"Oh yes. My attorney is insisting he does, and she says no judge will sign a divorce decree that leaves a stay-at-home mother without any financial means.

Although if that bastard could get away with not paying alimony, he would. He's trying to say he doesn't make as much money as he does, but I took screenshots of our joint bank account."

"That was good thinking."

"Oh, I didn't think of it. It was my attorney's suggestion. She is a fucking shark.

"There's a lot of paperwork we have to file. All our income, tax returns, debts. That jerk just bought a new Lexus. Thank God I won't have to help him pay that off now."

"There's one good thing!" Ravyn said, trying to make Julie laugh.

"My attorney even told me to take both girls to another counselor. They need it. They are having trouble in school."

"I'm sorry. I'm glad you are getting them some counseling."

"Yes. And it can help in my divorce case – that he's disrupted their lives. My attorney gave me a great recommendation. The girls have gone twice now, and I think it's helping."

"Is Rob still being an asshole?"

"Of course. But he has moved into the guest bedroom. At least I don't have to listen to him snore anymore. It does look like he'll buy me out of the house, so I've called one of my tennis buddies. She's a real estate agent specializing in corporate apartments and she's trying to help me identify three-bedroom apartments in the Buckhead area. They are really expensive."

"I remember. I couldn't afford to buy in Midtown and the rental prices were pretty steep a year ago."

"They aren't any lower now."

"What are you going to do?"

"I may have to rent OTP," Julie said, using the Atlanta phrase to refer to "Outside the Perimeter," or in the suburbs.

"Oh no. I just can't see you outside of Buckhead."

"I'd cry if I had to move too far out. I have my tennis club, the girls have their tennis practice, and they go to Walden Academy," Julie said, referring to a private preparatory school just north of Buckhead. "We could move to the Smyrna area. That wouldn't be too bad, but we'll have to see what apartments I find."

"Would you consider buying?"

"I'd like to rent first, see if I like my new neighborhood and neighbors. Plus, that's what my attorney recommends. I'll have to establish credit, get a job, and save for a down payment. She's even put me in touch with a financial planner. I need to update my will, get a budget in place, that kind of stuff. There's a lot to learn! And it's so overwhelming."

"I'm glad she's helping you. I hope I never need her but keep her contact info," Ravyn joked.

"She is. But did I mention how much I hate Rob? He did this. Couldn't keep his dick in his pants."

"I hate him too. I really do. You don't deserve this or him."

The friends were quiet for a moment. Then Julie said, "Well fuck him."

Ravyn barked out a laugh. "Yes, fuck him. I know this is awful, Julie. But I really believe you and the girls will be better off. I mean, what sort of male role model does he give your daughters?"

"He's such an asshole! Honestly, he's not giving them a very good role model. In time, I think they'll see that, but for now, they are devastated that their father is divorcing me. I feel like I did something wrong. That's hard to deal with."

Julie began to cry and Rayvn tried to be comforting, but she had no idea what to tell her friend. She had no idea how that would feel. Her parents were still married. Marc's parents were still married. And she dreaded the thought that Marc would ever leave her.

She'd probably feel just as devastated and Julie did right now, Ravyn thought.

They pulled into the valet at Del Frisco Grille and Julie dabbed her eyes, careful not to ruin her mascara.

"How bad do I look?" Julie asked as they got out of the car.

"You look wonderful."

"Be honest."

"If you keep your sunglasses on until you get to the bathroom everyone will think you are a celebrity, and we'll get a better table."

Julie gave Ravyn a small smile. "I'll head to the bathroom while you get our table."

Julie and Ravyn enjoyed their lunch. They ordered a bottle of wine and made a meal of mushroom flatbread, an order of cheesesteak egg rolls, and ahi tuna tacos.

Julie talked mostly about how her daughters were doing (not well), how her apartment hunting was going (not well), and how her mediation for the divorce was going (not well).

"Rob is just being difficult," Julie complained. "I mean he is the one seeking the divorce, but he's acting like I'm the one who wronged him. He's not even being civil anymore. Even though we are in the same house, we mostly text each other. We're barely speaking."

"That's terrible. I'm sorry he's being so childish."

"You know, I think he has always been this way, but I was so in love with him that I put up with it. I'm not doing that anymore. I'll fix dinner for me and the girls, but he's on his own. When he's not out to dinner with his homewrecker, he's ordering a lot of takeout. And he leaves his dirty takeout boxes all over the kitchen, just to be an ass."

"He's a complete jerk," Ravyn said.

"I'm not doing his laundry anymore, either. I don't even think he knows how to use the washing machine. I think he just takes everything — including his dirty underwear — to have it cleaned at a drop-off laundromat. Suits me. I don't want to touch his filthy things."

"This all sounds so stressful."

"It is. He's probably anxious to get me and the girls out of there so that homewrecker can move in and start taking care of him again."

"Do you think that's what he wants? For her to move in with him?"

"I'm sure of it. When he does speak, it's to tell me she'll be living in the house with him as soon as I'm gone."

Julie began to cry softly at the table. Ravyn reached over to hold her friend's hand.

"I'm so sorry."

Julie waved her free hand in front of her face. "That's why I'm glad I have a great friend like you. I don't know if I could make it without you. Thanks for listening. I know I've been blabbering too much about the divorce."

"No, no," Ravyn protested. "I want to be here for you, and I want to listen. You've done more than your fair share of listening to me complain."

"Well, tell me what's going on with you, with Harper, with Marc."

"Harper is close to saying her first word. She's been babbling. I think she's going to say dada. Marc thinks she'll say mama. We'll see. But we both hear her in the baby monitor, kind of cooing, kind of singing. She's being very vocal."

"That's exciting! You always remember their first word. Both my girls said mama first. Thank God."

"I just pray she says her first word at home and not at daycare."

"Listen, even if she says it at daycare, she'll say it for you and Marc at home, too. And trust me, once they start talking it's hard to get them to be quiet."

Ravyn laughed. "Yeah, then Marc and I will have to watch our language. It's not that we curse, but if one of us stubs a toe we can say some choice words. I don't want Harper suddenly parroting that to the daycare workers."

"Oh right. Lexie said 'shit' at her pre-school, and I thought I'd die. They called me at home to tell me what she'd said. I was embarrassed, but I'd been saying it around the house forever. I had to clean up my mouth after that."

"Marc curses far more than I do, so I'll have to get onto him about that."

"And how *is* Marc these days?"

"He's really sorry about what's happening to you."

"Thank you."

"I think if he ever meets up with Rob again, he'll punch him out for you."

"Tell him not to waste his energy. I don't want to have to bail Marc out of jail for that asshole."

"Right. I've already done that once."

"Oh, God, that's right. That Mexican jail."

Ravyn shook her head, not wanting to remember her having to bribe the Mexican police with her engagement ring to get Marc out of jail on trumped-up charges.

"Marc was being really attentive after you announced your divorce, but he's kind of gone back to having me do all the housework, grocery shopping, caring for Harper. It's exhausting."

"Motherhood is exhausting. I'm sorry he's not helping more. He seemed like a more modern father than Rob. Rob didn't do anything. Which is how I ended up a stay-at-home mother. I don't know how you do it working full time."

"Well, we kind of need the two jobs. I mean, Marc makes a good salary, but he's still paying off the loan to his father for all the money he borrowed to keep LindMark going. I know he was relieved to sell to Black Kat Investors."

"Didn't he make a bunch with the sale?"

"He certainly made a profit, but his father was charging interest on those loans that he took out years ago," Ravyn said, flatly. "There was a lot of interest. A lot."

"Oh. I didn't know that."

"My father-in-law is a rather cold man. Hard to warm up to. My mother-in-law is a darling. But her husband is... well, I'm sure she loves him and I'm sure he has some good qualities that she loves."

"But you don't see it."

"I don't see it."

Julie reached over and took Ravyn's hand. "Thanks for this. I needed to vent and to have a good time. Thank you."

"Listen, it was my pleasure. It got me out of the house for an afternoon and into an adult conversation. I'm getting just a little tired of reading 'Good Night, Moon' or asking Harper if she wants applesauce with her turkey dinner." Ravyn laughed. "She never answers, although she makes baby noises. I should enjoy it while I can. She can't complain!"

"But otherwise, you and Marc are OK? In the sack?"

"We've reconnected, but it's not the same. We are both so tired all the time."

"That's to be expected. Hang in there. It gets better."

Ravyn got home to find Marc asleep on the couch and Harper in her playpen in the middle of the living room. Harper stood up in her playpen and put her arms up, wanting to be picked up.

"OK, baby girl. Let me put down my bag," Ravyn said.

She put down her handbag and picked up her daughter, twirling her around the living room like they were dancing. Marc awoke with a start.

"Did I fall asleep? Where's Harper?"

"She's right here, dancing with me."

Marc sat up, sleepy eyed with his brown hair tousled and his shirt wrinkled. At that moment, Ravyn thought she knew what Marc must have looked like as a young boy.

Ravyn continued to dance with Harper in her arms. Harper squealed and laughed her baby giggle, which made Marc and Ravyn laugh as well.

"She has the cutest laugh," Marc said. "I love that laugh. The most beautiful sound."

"I agree. If she's happy, my heart is happy."

Marc got up and began to dance around his wife and daughter. He was doing a cross of the funky chicken and Steve Martin's King Tut moves. Harper just squealed louder. Ravyn didn't think she could be any happier.

Chapter 5

Fall in Atlanta meant only one thing: college football. Marc managed to get tickets to a University of Georgia football game and Ravyn packed up everything for an afternoon at Sanford Stadium in Athens, Georgia. Marc had graduated from UGA, and he and Ravyn always had a friendly wager whenever the Georgia Bulldogs played the Missouri Tigers. Ravyn had graduated with a journalism degree from Mizzou, and it wasn't until relatively recently that the two teams were in the same football conference, so they played each other once a year.

Georgia usually won the game, and Ravyn always tried to keep the wager within reason. Usually, the bet was something sexual. Ravyn felt like they both won no matter the losing team.

This time, Georgia was playing Vanderbilt. Ravyn was a little uncertain about bringing Harper to the game. What if she was fussy, or didn't like the noise or the crowds? What if they had to leave early?

Ravyn expressed all these fears to Marc as they loaded the Honda CR-V.

"We'll leave if she's unhappy," Marc said.

"But that will make you unhappy. You are going to want to see the game. If she's fussy I can leave the game, go to a cafe or restaurant and come get you when the game is over."

"We can leave together," Marc said.

"You know it pains me that I put her in a Georgia Bulldogs outfit," Ravyn said.

"I just want her to fit in. You have plenty of Mizzou outfits for her. And you put her in those all the time. This time it's my turn," Marc said, smiling.

In the end, Harper wasn't fazed at all by the noise or the crowds. She fell asleep in her mother's arms while Marc cheered and groaned as the game progressed. The final score was Vanderbilt 17, Georgia 16 in a heartbreaker for the Georgia fans.

"I just can't believe that game," Marc exclaimed as they were shoulder to shoulder with other fans exiting the game. "We should have won it."

"I'm glad we didn't have to leave. It was a close one," Ravyn agreed.

"I appreciate your cheering for Georgia."

"I support your team, as long as it is not playing *my* team," Ravyn said.

"Traffic is going to be slow getting back to Atlanta. Do you want to stop at a restaurant in Athens?"

"Sure. Any chance to eat out is fine by me."

"Did you bring extra baby food for Harper?" he asked.

"Is the pope Catholic? I've always got extra. Although we could order some mac and cheese and she'd probably eat that."

"Sounds great. I'll take you to one of my favorite haunts when I was in college."

"Is it still here?"

"Of course, it is. It's the Varsity!"

"Baby, I don't think Harper can eat anything on that menu."

"Well, she can have her baby food and we can have a glorified steak or a heavyweight," Marc said, using the lingo of the Varsity orders. "It sounds cool instead of just a hamburger or a hot dog with extra chili, doesn't it?"

"We'll probably both have heartburn tonight."

"No, we'll be fine."

As they sat down at a table, their trays loaded with a couple of hamburgers, onion rings, French fries, Marc tore off a small piece of his hamburger and gave it to Harper. She began to eat it, then made a face and spit it out.

"It might have had some mustard on it," Ravyn said. "Scrape off the condiments and give her a little."

Marc tried again, but Harper wasn't having any of it.

"Oh Harper, you don't know what you are missing!"

"No, I think she does. I'm sorry she's not interested in your college fare."

"God, I ate here so much when I was at school. It was cheap and fast."

"Sounds like Shakespeare's for me at Mizzou."

"Was that a burger place?"

"No, that was The Heidelberg. Shakespeare's is a pizza place."

"Are they both still on campus?"

"They are. Although The Heidelberg burned a few years back. After I had graduated. But they rebuilt it."

"What do you want to do for Thanksgiving? My mother is asking if we want to spend it with them in Dunwoody," Marc said.

"You know my parents are going to ask the same question. I suppose we'll have to figure out how we want to handle the holidays. Both families are going to want to see us. Or rather, they'll want to see Harper."

Marc smiled with a mouthful of hamburger and nodded. He wiped his mouth with his paper napkin before he said, "Yeah. They will. It's kind of not fair that my parents are close and can see Harper more. Maybe we should go see your folks for Thanksgiving."

"That might mean we're at your parents' house for Christmas. My folks might not like that," Ravyn said. "It's Harper's first Christmas."

"Our parents really don't live that far apart," he said. "Maybe we could do Thanksgiving with my parents on Thursday and then spend part of the weekend with your parents."

"That might work."

"And I'd really rather not spend that much time with my family. I mean, Brooke won't be there for Thanksgiving so it will just be my parents, Bruce, and us. It can always get a little volatile."

"I'm sure it will be fine," Ravyn said. "Bruce has been doing well. He's got a job now, right? He's not drinking or using drugs."

"But we never know when that will change."

Marc was thoughtful for a moment. "Hey, what if we ditched our parents for Thanksgiving and went to St. Simons, to the King & Prince, like we did for our honeymoon?"

Ravyn's eyes got wide. "Oh my God. That would be great!"

"We didn't get to do anything for our anniversary this year since you and Harper were sick. We could do a little weekend getaway. I'm sure our parents would understand."

"Honey, we'd better make reservations right now. We might not get a room."

"When we get home, we'll see if anything is available. If not, we'll split the time between our families."

"Deal."

Julie asked Ravyn if she could pick up the girls from their school on the following Monday, the day of her mediation session for her divorce. She expected she and Rob would take longer than school hours to hammer out the divorce details.

"Of course," Ravyn replied. "I'll take a half-day off and pick up Harper, then get the girls. Harper would probably love to have some playmates. I know the girls are older, but Harper just loves attention."

"I'm sure my girls will fawn all over Harper. They'll probably want to dress her up like a doll. I hope she's ready for that."

"Why don't you plan on coming over after it's done and have dinner with us. Marc usually goes to the gym on Monday evenings, so we can have some girl chat."

"I don't want to put you out," Julie said.

"Listen, you aren't going to want to fix dinner so let me. I'll even open a bottle of Star 1 wine. Kyle Quitman sent us a case when Harper was born. I thought it was an odd gift, but now that I'm not nursing as much, I realize it was a fabulous gift. I can make some chili and we'll have the Cabernet. It's just so good."

"OK, you've convinced me. I don't know how long we will be, though."

"It's chili. It can stay on the stove until you get here. If I need to, I'll feed all three girls earlier and park them in front of a movie. Harper just loves the movie Monsters Inc. I think it's all the colorful monsters."

"My girls loved that movie, too. I'm sure they'll watch it with Harper."

"Great. I'll see you when you get here on Monday."

Julie knocked on Ravyn's front door around seven in the evening on the Monday of her long mediation session.

Ravyn opened the door to her friend, whom she could see had been crying. Ravyn immediately hugged Julie.

"Are the girls around?" Julie whispered.

"I've already fed them, and they are watching the movie."

"Let me go say hello and then we can chat."

"I'll pour you some wine. You look like you need it."

"I need the whole bottle, but a glass will be a good start."

Julie went into the guest room and her daughters jumped up to hug their mother. She explained that their father would be moving out of the house until the divorce was final. They'd then have to move into an apartment, so they'd all have to start packing up their belongings. The girls would keep their bedroom furniture and all their clothes and toys.

But they'd all be moving in the next month or so, she explained.

"I hate daddy," Ashley said.

"Let's try not to use that word," Julie said. "Let's try to say we don't like his actions, but let's not say we hate him."

"But I do hate him," she replied, bursting into tears.

"I know this is hard, sweetheart," Julie said, hugging her oldest daughter. At almost 14, Ashley was clearly an early teen with the emotions to match. "It's hard for me too. And we don't want to cry and upset Harper."

Julie pulled a facial tissue out of her handbag and wiped Ashley's tears.

"Can you watch the rest of the movie with her? I'll have dinner with Ravyn and then we'll all go home. Your daddy won't be at the house when we get home."

Ravyn had overheard the conversation and handed Julie a glass of wine as soon as she came out of the guest room.

Julie took a long drink. "Wow. This is good."

"Are you hungry at all?"

"I honestly wasn't until I walked in and smelled that chili. I didn't eat at all today. Too nervous and upset. But now my mouth is watering."

"Let's get it served up and just sit down and relax."

Ravyn had also baked some cornbread to go with the chili and the two friends sat at the small bistro breakfast table to enjoy their meal.

"I overheard you tell the girls Rob is moving out temporarily."

"Yes, thank God! My attorney insisted on it since we don't have an apartment finalized. I've got one that I've looked at. It's a three-bedroom, two-bath. It's a bit small. Only 1,500 square feet. My house is nearly four times that! I think the girls are going to have to get used to a smaller place and share a bathroom. They are going to be unhappy that they don't have their own bathrooms at the new place."

"Gosh, that is small. Even this place is 2,100 square feet and sometimes I think it's small for us. I can't imagine two teen girls. I'm going to have to buy you a referee outfit and a whistle."

Julie smiled. "You might have to. The apartment is running my credit check and I've put down a security deposit, but we won't be able to move in until December 1, if we get it."

"What will you do if you don't get it? Where will you go?"

"My friend who is helping me find the apartments said it really should just be a formality. After the divorce in a few weeks, the judge will likely sign the decree saying we can live in the house until we can move into the apartment. We should be in our new place in time for Christmas. What a Christmas this will be!"

"Are the divorce terms favorable for you?"

"My attorney did well. I'll get child support and alimony. The child support will cover the apartment rent and most of the tuition for Walden. Rob will get the girls every other weekend and two weeks during summer break and every other major holiday. He didn't even fight to have them in a 50/50 custody split. I'll have the girls this Christmas. I insisted. He didn't put up a fight, at all. Not at all for the girls. He just wants us out so he can move that homewrecker in."

"I hate to even ask where he's going until he can move back to the house."

"Where do you think he's going? He's moving in with her!"

"Does she have a house?"

"An apartment. Why the hell couldn't he move in with her permanently? Why am I going to be in an apartment, and she'll be in my house?" Julie began to cry, then wiped her eyes with her napkin and drained her wine glass.

"More?" Ravyn asked, holding up the bottle.

"Just one. I've got to drive home, and I can't stay late. I'm exhausted."

"This has to be emotionally draining."

"It is. But I'm glad it is nearly over. The place we're planning to rent has a pool, so the girls will be excited about that, at least."

"Pools make everything better. You know Harper and I will be visiting as soon as the pool opens next summer."

"You better! If I'm paying nearly $3,000 for 1,500 square feet, we are having pool parties as much as we can."

Ravyn was relieved when Julie called to say she had been approved for the new apartment and was starting to box up some breakables she wanted to take. Ravyn laughed when Julie said she'd really like to leave Rob just two plates, two glasses, and one fork, but she was splitting the dishes and cutlery evenly.

Julie did admit she was cleaning the shower grout and behind the toilet with Rob's toothbrush. "Don't worry, I'll throw it out," she said. "Maybe."

"Marc and I can help you with the move if you need it."

"I'm hiring movers. My attorney even got Rob to pay for it. I tell you, she thought of everything. She's a shark."

"Marc and I will be out of town over Thanksgiving weekend, but we can help when we get back. You're still moving into the apartment on December 1?"

"Yes, and thank you. You're out of town over the holiday?"

"We decided we needed a little getaway. You know Harper and I were sick for our first anniversary. We're going back to St. Simons and staying at the King and Prince."

"That will be wonderful for you. Is Harper going? If you two want to go alone, I'd be happy to watch her. I'll have two helpers."

"Thanks, but we are going as a family. And I don't know that I could be away from Harper that long."

"I understand. But my offer stands if you change your mind. Maybe a couple's weekend is just what you and Marc need."

"We do. But we've rented a two-bedroom suite, so Harper will be in her own bedroom."

"That sounds wonderful. What did your parents say about not visiting them for Thanksgiving? And his parents?"

"Neither side was all that happy, but they understood. And we'll split the Christmas vacation between the two families. I'm glad they don't live that far away."

Ravyn, Marc, and Harper arrived at the King and Prince Resort, where Marc and Ravyn had spent their honeymoon the year before, the day before

Baby Steps

Thanksgiving. They had also found a nanny through the hotel to help with Harper.

Marc and Ravyn booked a couples massage and Chloe, the nanny, took Harper for a few hours so they could enjoy their spa day. Chloe had been so delightful, they ended up hiring her for nearly the whole long holiday weekend.

Chloe was a nursing student at the College of Coastal Georgia in Brunswick. She knew infant CPR and Ravyn was relieved to know that.

Chloe planned to get her core classes at the local college, then transfer to another college to get her Bachelor of Nursing degree. Marc, of course, tried to talk up the University of Georgia, but Chloe said she'd probably transfer to Georgia Southern University in Statesboro. It was closer to home, she told him.

On Thanksgiving Day, Marc, Ravyn, and Chloe, with Harper in her stroller, stood in line at the enormous Thanksgiving buffet. Marc and Ravyn loaded their plates with shrimp, crab legs, and other seafood delicacies, as well as turkey, mashed potatoes, and other traditional fixings.

Chloe got nearly all Marc and Ravyn did but added some extra mashed potatoes. She just bet Harper would like that. Chloe also had organic baby food just in case Harper didn't.

The threesome sat at a table and Chloe took one bite of her food before she fed a hungry Harper in a hotel high chair. Harper's little mouth came open as the spoon came close to her.

Harper gobbled up the mashed potatoes. Then small bites of pureed turkey, apple, and sweet potatoes went into Harper's mouth until she grabbed for the spoon to try to feed herself.

With Chloe there, Marc and Ravyn got to enjoy their meal as well. When they finished eating, Chloe took Harper up to the hotel room while Marc and Ravyn walked hand in hand along the beach all the way to the St. Simons Island lighthouse.

They had to turn around before the tide came in and blocked their way back to the resort.

Marc and Ravyn were like two lovebirds when they got back to the hotel and paid Chloe for her time that day. The couple was grateful for her help with Harper. Chloe said Harper was an angel compared to a few children she'd minded at the resort.

Marc and Ravyn fell into their bed and made love for the first time in a long time. And Harper slept through the night, giving the married couple a long lie-in.

Marc rolled over in the king bed and felt Ravyn's soft naked body. Marc's penis began to rise.

Ravyn moaned and rolled over toward Marc, snuggling in toward him. Marc pulled Ravyn toward him.

Marc rolled over on Ravyn as they began to make love. They kissed deeply before Marc began to work down to Ravyn's breasts, still larger because of the baby. Ravyn gasped as he worked her nipples, which were still sensitive.

Marc then began to work his kisses down Ravyn's stomach and to her vagina. He began working her clitoris and Ravyn groaned with pleasure.

Ravyn rose out of the bed and reached for her husband's stiff shaft, taking it in her mouth and taking it deep in her throat. Marc groaned his own pleasure at having his wife deep throat his dick.

As both got closer to climaxing, Marc climbed on top of Ravyn and bent her legs, penetrating deep inside her. Before long, the couple was climaxing together. Marc collapsed on top of Ravyn, and both fell soundly asleep.

In what felt like only moments later, Harper began to wail, hungry. Ravyn dragged herself out of bed, grabbed her robe, and padded into the in-suite kitchen, and grabbed some organic baby food for Harper.

She put Harper in a portable high chair, got out a rubber spoon, and began to feed Harper. When Harper began to spit out the rest of her food, Ravyn twisted the cap back on her food and tried to lay her back down, but Harper was up and ready to play.

Ravyn took Harper out to the balcony, putting her into her portable playpen. Harper was pulling herself up and walking around the insides of the playpen.

They could hear the waves coming onto the beach. It was hypnotic and relaxing. Ravyn looked down to see her daughter rubbing her eyes, getting sleepy again.

Ravyn, her own eyes getting heavy, continued to listen to the waves and looked over again to see Harper had fallen asleep.

She didn't want to disturb her, so just let her sleep, but texted Marc she was out on the balcony. Then she closed her eyes to enjoy the sound of the waves.

Marc slid the glass door open. "I wondered where you had gone."

"Harper ate and then was up, so we came out here so we wouldn't disturb you. There's a nice breeze this morning. And it's so warm! Not like Atlanta. I'm going to hate to leave. It feels like we just got here."

"We did," Marc said, sitting in the chair next to Ravyn. "It's always too short. If you want to take a shower, I'll sit out here with her for a while."

"Oh, thank you, Marc. I never knew having an infant meant taking five-minute showers."

"Wait until she's walking."

"Don't remind me. She's starting to really rock back and forth on her hands and knees, so crawling won't be far behind. And she's pulling herself up in the playpen. We need to baby-proof the house soon."

"We'll get to it," Marc said, taking Ravyn by the hand.

Baby Steps

The couple sat outside for another half hour, watching the waves, and enjoying the early morning sunshine.

Julie had the movers arrive shortly after she dropped her daughters off at Walden. By the end of the day, they'd be moved into their new apartment. Julie couldn't help crying as the boxes were loaded onto the moving truck. She was leaving the home she'd had for the past 10 years.

She'd decorated the home and filled it with love. She cursed Rob. She hated him more than ever. She knew he was champing at the bit to move back into the house. She'd left a few unpleasant surprises for him. She hoped he didn't find them right away.

Ravyn came over to her new place with takeout Chinese. She wanted Julie and her girls to enjoy a meal without having to cook or clean up. Ravyn even brought a bottle of white wine for the adults to enjoy and some Sprite for the girls.

"You didn't bring Harper?"

"Marc's got daddy duty tonight. I can use a break, too. I like your new place. It's small, but you'll make it cozy."

"Well, I already realize not all of the furniture will fit in the girls' rooms. We may have to bring it back to the house."

"Oh no. I wish we could store it for you, but we're out of space for storage, too."

"I mean, I could try to sell it, but I probably wouldn't get much for a single dresser or a vanity set."

"Probably not."

"Did I tell you my exciting news? I'm going to study for my real estate license."

"Oh, Julie, I think you'd be great at that."

"And that's the best part," Julie said, her eyes bright. "My real estate friend said she could hire me to stage houses for sale. I don't need a license for that. So, I'd be making some money while I study for my exam. And I'd be able to set my own hours, so I could still drop off and pick up the girls at school."

"That's great! I know you'll do well with that. Your house was always so well decorated."

"I'm probably going to take a course on flower decorating, too, so I can do those fancy arrangements you see in high-end homes. We can offer that as a service and save money for the client. And I can also do that for staging. I can do it right away."

Ravyn stood up and hugged Julie. "I'm so happy for you. I think you'll be so good at real estate and staging those homes. You're a natural. You could sell ice cubes to Eskimos."

"I'm not sure about that. But I'm excited. I really think this is a career for me that will allow me to make my own money and set my own hours. I can definitely see why working mothers get into real estate."

Julie chatted excitedly about starting December 11 with her friend's agency in Buckhead, to get a walk-through and learn what homes she'd need to stage that week.

Unfortunately, the women were interrupted by an argument between Julie's daughters over the bathroom.

"I want in first! I'm the oldest!" Ashley shouted at her sister.

"But you take too long! I need in now!" Lexie shouted back.

Julie stood up and clapped her hands. "Girls! Girls! You have to share this bathroom. Don't make me have to set up a schedule!"

"Mom, I need in there now. It's an emergency," Ashley said. She loudly whispered, "I have my period."

"Lexie, why do you need in first?"

"I need to pee."

"OK, Lexie, you go in my bathroom and Ashley you go in yours. But you are going to have to learn to share."

"I hate this place!" Lexie shouted. "I hate my room and I hate sharing!" She slammed the door to the master bathroom.

"Well, I'm sure we're making a great impression on the new neighbors," Julie said to Ravyn.

"Do you need to go talk to her? I'll wait."

"No. The counselor said she's going to have these temper tantrums. It's like I've got a toddler again."

"Change is hard. I know you are doing your best and I'm sure Lexie will learn to love it. Did you show them the pool?"

Julie smiled. "I did. We can see it from our balcony."

Ravyn and Julie went out onto the small balcony. The pool deck lights glowed below them, but the pool was covered. The pool had closed for the winter.

Julie had set up two small wicker chairs and a mosaic-tiled bistro table out on the balcony. Ravyn stepped back into the apartment and got their wine glasses and the wine, placing them carefully on the table.

They sat in silence, darkness enveloping them. Music drifted in the air from a nearby apartment.

After a while, Rayvn broke the silence. "This will be your little haven, won't it?"

"I'm sure it will be, especially when the girls get on my last nerve. I think that will be often since we'll be on top of each other."

Julie sipped her wine as a tear slipped down her cheek.

Baby Steps

"I know it will get better," Julie said, "but right now it's awful for all of us."

"It will get better, Julie. I just know it will."

Ravyn reached over in the dark and held her friend's hand. Julie gave Ravyn's hand a squeeze and nodded.

Chapter 6

Julie and her daughters got into their new routine at their apartment. Julie got the girls ready for school, dropping them off before she went to the real estate office to see if she had any homes to stage.

If she didn't have any work for the company, she studied for her real estate exam. She found it empowering to be learning so much and be making a bit of money on her own.

Julie bought a small artificial tree, a few ornaments, lights and decorated her home for Christmas. At night, after the girls were done with homework, fed, and in bed, Julie sat with a glass of wine and sat in front of the Christmas tree in the dark. Sometimes she cried. Other times, she just sat on the couch and enjoyed the stillness.

Ravyn and Marc bought a live tree, but set it up in the playpen, pulling up the sides to protect it from a crawling Harper, and prayed Felix, Ravyn's gray tomcat, wouldn't try to climb it.

All the breakable ornaments were placed high on the tree, with the plastic ones toward the bottom, which every morning Ravyn found scattered on the floor of the playpen thanks to Felix. He clearly was jumping in and knocking them off the tree.

White flashing lights were strung among the pine branches. The tree made the whole house smell good.

Ravyn had invited Julie and her girls over for Christmas Eve dinner that year. She and Marc planned to have dinner with his parents on Christmas Day, then head up to South Carolina to spend a few days with her parents.

"I know you probably wanted to spend Christmas Eve with just us, Marc, but I didn't want Julie to spend part of the holiday alone with the girls in that apartment. It's really small."

"No, I think it's great she's coming. Harper loves her girls. It's cute to see her around them."

Baby Steps

Julie and the girls arrived around five o'clock Christmas Eve. Ravyn's office had closed at noon that afternoon so she could get Harper and the shopping done before everyone arrived.

Ravyn had put a turkey breast in the oven, made mashed potatoes and a green bean casserole. Julie brought a pumpkin pie and some ice cream for dessert.

They sat around the wooden dining room table, the adults having some wine, and the girls having sparkling cider. Harper had her water in a sippy cup.

Lexie and Ashley took turns feeding her mashed potatoes and small pieces of turkey and gravy, even small pieces of green beans. Harper grinned at both girls as they fussed over her. Harper loved the attention.

After dinner, they had pumpkin pie and vanilla ice cream. Ravyn also pulled out some freshly made whipped cream to top the pie.

"I'm stuffed," Marc said, patting his stomach. "I'm going to have to hit the gym hard after the holidays."

"Girls, I have Rudolph the Red-Nosed Reindeer to watch with Harper if you want," Ravyn said. "I know it's probably too young for you, but I think she'll like that movie. I have it on demand. I also have Santa Claus is Comin' to Town and Frosty the Snowman."

"No, we like those shows," Ashley said.

"It's all set up in the guest bedroom," Ravyn said. "Just push the play button on the remote."

Lexie and Ashley each grabbed one of Harper's hands and helped her "walk" into the guest bedroom to watch the holiday classics.

"Can I get you another glass of wine? Or maybe a decaf coffee?" Ravyn asked Marc and Julie.

"I'll take a scotch, Ravyn," Marc said.

"I'd like another glass of wine, if you have it," Julie said. "Don't open a bottle just for me, though."

"We've got another bottle chilling. It's good, isn't it?" Ravyn said, heading into the kitchen for the new bottle of wine. Marc stood up and got his scotch, then sat back down on the brown leather couch. "And don't worry, I want another glass, too. I'm opening it for both of us."

Felix came out of Harper's room and gave a small meow.

"Hey Felix," Ravyn said. "Do you want your dinner, too?"

"How's Felix with Harper?" Julie asked as Ravyn poured a glass of wine for Julie and herself, then got the kibble for Felix's food bowl.

"We were a little worried at first. Felix kept jumping up into the crib and I was afraid he'd get too close to her face and smother her. We kept him out of Harper's room as much as we could. But as she got older, Felix started sleeping with her in the crib, cuddled up right next to her. It's cute to see now. She puts her arm on him as she sleeps. He's really very tolerant of her."

"That's wonderful. My girls are begging for a kitten," Julie said. "Rob always disliked animals in the house. Claimed he was allergic." Julie rolled her eyes. "You know his whore has a dog, don't you? That dog is going to move into my house!"

"Really?"

"Yes. That mutt is going to move into my house, and the dog will, too," Julie gave a quick laugh. Even Marc smiled at the joke.

"But are you getting a kitten?" Ravyn asked.

"I'm thinking about it," Julie said. "I'll have to pay a pet deposit at the apartment. Quite frankly, I'd like to wait and make the girls earn money through chores to help pay for the deposit and adoption fee. The adoption fee isn't much, but the girls need to show me they are responsible enough to take care of a pet. I don't want to be the one to take care of it by myself."

"I'd recommend one of the rescue organizations. They often have free or reduced-cost adoption events," Ravyn said. "And you can get an older cat. I love kittens. I got Felix as a kitten, but they are a handful. Older cats are calmer."

"I agree with all of that, but the girls are dead set on a kitten," Julie said, taking a sip of her wine. "We'll see. Nothing will happen before the end of the year. If I play my cards right, I'll say we have to wait until the end of school when they can spend a lot of time with the kitten over the summer. That gives me about six months."

Ravyn, Marc, and Julie chatted for about another hour, but then Julie looked at her watch and realized the time.

"Oh! I've got to get the girls home. I still haven't put out their Christmas gifts from Santa, and I need to get them in bed."

"They don't still believe in Santa, do they?"

"They don't," Julie replied, laughing. "But they keep quiet about it because they get an extra gift."

Ravyn opened the guest bedroom and found all the girls, Harper included, sound asleep on the guest bed. Ashley and Lexie were on either side of the infant to keep her from rolling off the bed.

Julie smiled when she saw the girls asleep. "I hate to wake them. They look so peaceful."

"They do," Ravyn agreed. "Any other night I'd say let them sleep here. But I know you'll want them at home for Christmas morning."

Julie walked over and began to rub Lexie's back. "Lexie, sweetie, wake up." Then she reached over to rub Ashley's arm. "Ashley, time to wake up. We need to go home."

"What?" Lexie asked sleepily. She raised up from the bed, confused. "Did we see the movies?"

"I think you fell asleep, honey," Ravyn said, picking up Harper, who was dead weight. Harper was out like a light. "I'll put Harper in her crib. Don't leave before I come out."

Ravyn got her daughter undressed and into her sleeper without too much fuss. Harper began to cry, but Marc came into the nursery, motioned for Ravyn to say good night to Julie, then rubbed Harper's head until she went back to sleep.

Julie had both girls in their coats by the front door when Ravyn came out of Harper's room.

"Can I send you home with any leftovers?" Ravyn asked. "The rest of the pie or ice cream?"

"No, that's fine," Julie began to say.

"Mom, the ice cream?" Lexie asked.

"OK, the ice cream," Julie conceded.

Ravyn got the leftover ice cream out of the freezer, put it in a plastic bag, and handed it to Lexie. She also packed up the pie and put that in another plastic bag, handing it to Ashley.

"What do you say?" Julie asked her daughters.

"Thank you, Auntie Ravyn," Lexie and Ashley said.

"You're welcome. You'll want pie with that ice cream. Enjoy."

"Thanks again for dinner tonight. It was great to see you."

When their guests left, Ravyn and Marc began to clean the kitchen, loading the dishwasher and starting it before heading to bed.

"Are you ready for Harper's first Christmas?" Marc asked.

"Be sure to put out some cookies and a glass of milk."

"You know she won't understand all that."

"Well, just take some bites out of the cookies and drink some of the milk."

"I always wanted to play Santa Claus," Marc laughed, taking half a bite of the cookie, and replacing it on a plate. "Now I am going to have to hit the gym."

"You want to play Santa?" Ravyn asked, playfully swatting at him with the dish towel. "I'd like to jingle your bells."

Marc grinned and chased Ravyn into the master bedroom.

Ravyn and Marc awoke to Harper's babbling in the baby monitor. "Guess our girl is up."

"At least she's not crying. I'll get her fed and then we can open the Christmas gifts."

"Sounds like a plan. I'm going to jump in the shower," Marc said.

"Save me some hot water," Ravyn said.

Ravyn got Harper out of her crib and fed her. She also started coffee.

Marc came out of the shower and told Ravyn he'd saved some hot water for her. "I'll finish feeding her. You go ahead and shower."

Ravyn could hear Marc making the airplane noises and Harper squealed her delight.

About thirty minutes later, Ravyn dressed Harper in a red and white outfit with "Harper's First Christmas" stitched on the front. She had ordered it online. She put a red headband with a red flower on her head. Harper's hair was light and wispy. Mostly she looked bald without some sort of headband.

She hoped her daughter's hair would eventually come in dark brown and wavy like Marc's hair, not fine and straight like her own light brown hair. She was pleased to see her daughter's eyes remained bright blue.

"Your daddy is going to have to lock you in the house and keep the teenaged boys out when you get older, beautiful girl," Ravyn whispered as she tickled Harper's belly. That elicited a giggle from Harper.

"There are my beautiful gals," Marc said as Ravyn brought Harper into the living room. Ravyn was wearing jeans with a holiday sweater.

Marc had on his khaki pants and a deep burgundy Henley shirt. Ravyn thought it looked great with his coloring.

Marc had started a fire in the fireplace. "I thought it would be more festive with a fire, and take the chill out of the house," he said. "Let's sit Harper in her high chair and give her a present. We might have to help her with the paper, rip it a little to get it started. I think she'll know what to do after that."

He put Harper's high chair in front of the Christmas tree and put a medium-sized box wrapped in reindeer paper on the high chair's tray and ripped a small corner of the gift. Harper proceeded to push the present off the tray.

"I hope that wasn't breakable," Ravyn said, frowning.

"What idiot would give an infant a breakable gift?" Marc replied.

"Well, it could be a Baby's First Christmas ornament. That might be breakable."

"Let's hope that it wasn't."

Marc put the gift back on the tray but kept his hand on it so Harper couldn't push it off again.

"Maybe you should just open it for her."

Marc conceded and ripped open the box to find, indeed, it *was* a Harper's First Christmas ornament with the year 2017 on it.

"You should have warned me. I'd have given her another gift," Marc said. "I didn't mean to call you an idiot. I didn't know you'd gotten this for her."

Ravyn smiled. "It's not broken, is it?"

"No. And let's hang it high up on the tree. If Felix breaks this one, I'll wring his neck."

"Put it up for now, but I'll box it up later today. I don't want it broken."

They took turns opening the rest of Harper's gifts, then turned to the gifts they had gotten each other.

Ravyn had purchased new boxing gloves for Marc, and a gift certificate to use with his favorite personal trainer, Joseph.

Marc had gotten Ravyn a pendant necklace with an "H" encrusted with genuine amethysts, the birthstone of February. Harper's birthstone.

"Oh, Marc, this is beautiful," Ravyn said, wiping a tear from her eye. "Thank you."

"I know you love sapphires, but I was hoping amethysts were a new favorite."

"Oh, they are!" Ravyn exclaimed, putting her new necklace on. "I'll wear it when we go to your parents' house for dinner."

"Well thank *you* for my new gloves and certificate training time with Joseph," he said. "You knew exactly what to get me."

Marc and Ravyn had a light lunch before packing up Ravyn's Honda CR-V and heading up to Marc's parents' home in Dunwoody.

Edward and Carol Linder's five-bedroom, four and a half bath two-story home felt like a mansion to Ravyn when she first met them at their home last year after she and Marc had gotten engaged. At nearly 3,200 square feet, the Linder home felt far bigger than Ravyn and Marc's more modest three-bedroom home.

Even their yard was bigger. Ravyn was certainly glad Marc didn't have to mow the yard, although she knew he did as a kid. The Linders now hired a service to take care of it.

Carol Linder always made Ravyn feel so welcome in the home, while Edward Linder was a standoffish and distant man.

"Let me see my granddaughter!" Carol exclaimed as they stood at the front door. Carol opened her arms wide, but Harper clung to Ravyn, turning her face away from her grandmother.

"She's gotten into this shy phase," Ravyn apologized. "She'll come around."

"That's just fine, Ravyn," Carol said, ushering the family in. "All babies go through that phase. Although Marc never did seem to have that phase. He was curious and into everything. I just knew he would take the world by storm."

Carol gave a smile to her oldest son, who blushed slightly.

"Where's Dad?" Marc asked.

"In the living room reading his book," Carol said. "Edward!" she called. "Marc, Ravyn, and Harper are here!"

Marc and Ravyn could hear muffled grumbling before Edward came into the foyer. "Take their jackets, Edward," Carol commanded. "Let's get you inside. Such crazy weather we're having this week. We've had the heat on in the morning and the air conditioning on in the afternoon."

"We had a fire going this morning," Ravyn said. "It's hard to guess how to dress Harper. I don't want her to be too hot or cold."

"Well, this little outfit is darling," Carol said.

Ravyn had dressed Harper in white tights with a burgundy velvet dress with white trim. She had a backup outfit in case this one got soiled.

"Will you come to Mimi?" Carol asked Harper, who finally reached her arms out and leaned toward her grandmother. "There's my darling girl," Carol said, taking Harper in her arms and placing her on her hip. "Let's see what Mimi is baking for dinner, shall we? I bet she has some sugar cookies for you."

Carol and Harper went off into the kitchen. Ravyn and Marc gave Edward their light jackets, and he placed them in the coat closet just inside the foyer.

"Come in," Edward said. "Will you join me for a drink?"

"Scotch for me," Marc said, eyeing his father, who looked tired.

"I'll wait until dinner, thank you," Ravyn said. "I'll go see if Carol needs help in the kitchen."

Marc followed his father into the living room's wet bar, while Ravyn headed down the hall to the kitchen.

"Are you feeling OK?" Marc asked his father.

"Of course. Why?"

"You look tired, that's all."

"Since when do you care about my health?"

Marc was sorry he had asked. His father always made him feel small lately and managed to put him down.

"Well, I can see you've been hitting the gym and keeping off the pounds."

"Listen, jackass. I don't need your smart mouth."

Marc took a long sip of his scotch. He was hoping he wouldn't be drunk before dinner was served.

"Do you need any help in here?" Ravyn asked.

"I've got the turkey in the oven, some casseroles ready for the microwave. If you want to peel the potatoes, that would be a big help."

"Great. Do you have an apron? I don't want to get my outfit dirty," Ravyn said.

Carol pulled out an apron from a kitchen drawer and handed it to her. It was a snowman apron from the neck down.

"This is so cute," Ravyn said. "I won't want to get this dirty either."

"Don't worry. It's washable. And I have more. I like having lots of Christmas-themed things," Carol said. "It's my favorite holiday."

Ravyn peeled potatoes as Carol basted the turkey. Harper was happily in an old wooden family high chair, banging on the tray with a wooden spoon.

"Has she said her first word yet?" Carol asked.

"I'm quite certain she said her first word at daycare, but we heard her say dada a few weeks ago."

"Were you disappointed she didn't say mama first?"

"Not at all. Honestly, Marc is such a great father. I really think he loves having a girl. I was a little afraid since I wasn't having a boy that he'd be disappointed."

"Disappointed? Why on earth would you think he'd be disappointed?"

"Well, a son would carry on the Linder name," Ravyn said.

"I'm sure my granddaughter will be just like you. You didn't take Marc's last name, so she might very well carry on the Linder name."

Ravyn was quiet. "Can I ask you something?"

"Sure."

"Does it bother you that I didn't take Marc's last name? That I'm still a Shaw?"

"Of course not. I envy you. I was raised that a woman married and took her husband's last name. I liked my maiden name. If I could, I would have kept it, too."

"Carol, what is your maiden name? I don't even know it."

"It's Roosevelt."

"Like the president?"

"Yes. We are distantly related."

"Oh my God! That's really interesting! My daughter is related to two presidents!"

"She sure is. Although we are on the Oyster Bay side of the family. Teddy's side. Franklin married Teddy's niece, you know."

"I didn't know. I need to get on Ancestry.com and get all this down for Harper. And Marc. This is just awesome. My family is from the Midwest. We don't have any celebrities on our family trees."

"It's really a distant celebrity. I hate to tell you how distant."

"It's OK. When I tell Harper, it will be kissing cousins! Hey, when is Bruce arriving?"

"He should be here after work."

"He had to work today? It's Christmas."

"He's been working at Northside Hospital. That is a 24/7 work environment."

"Is it a new job?" Ravyn asked. "I thought he was working in Midtown."

"He got this job a couple of months ago as a janitor in the hospital. Oh, I guess they call them sanitation workers. It's shift work, so I'm glad he'll be here. He worked the early shift today."

"I'm glad he's coming. He really saved the day with Harper's birth. He told you about that, didn't he?"

"He just said he drove you to the hospital. Is there more?"

"Oh my God, I can't believe he didn't tell you all of it."

"What's all of it?"

Ravyn recounted her panic of her contractions coming closer than she thought and Bruce driving her to the hospital, leaving out the part about him taking out their mailbox and then nearly passing out in the birthing suite.

"Bruce really is a good boy," Carol said, referring to her youngest son as if he was a small child.

"He really is," was all Ravyn could say.

Bruce arrived around five o'clock that evening, about an hour before the turkey was ready to come out of the oven.

Marc and his father had nursed their drinks in the living room in silence.

When Edward and Marc greeted Bruce, they had drinks in their hands. Bruce could smell the alcohol on their breath. It made Bruce want a drink so badly. Instead, he asked for a ginger ale.

Edward made a face at his younger son. He considered his addiction a failure on Bruce's part. Marc got his brother the soft drink. Marc also considered his younger brother's addiction a failure on his part but didn't make a face at his brother the way his father had.

Carol greeted her younger son warmly. Ravyn hugged Bruce as well.

"She's getting so big," Bruce said of his niece, who continued to bang the spoon on the high chair tray before throwing it on the floor.

"That's enough of that, young lady," Ravyn said, picking up the spoon and placing it in the sink.

Without her spoon, Harper began to fuss and cry.

"Are you getting hungry?" Ravyn asked her daughter. "Let's get you fed before the Christmas dinner. Maybe you'll play quietly during dinner."

Ravyn heated up some baby food in a small glass bowl. It was turkey with peas and carrots.

"Can I do it?" Bruce asked.

"Sure. I'm sure she'd love her uncle Bruce to feed her. Just make sure the food isn't too hot. Put it up to your lip. If it's too hot for your lip, it's too hot for her."

Bruce pulled a dining chair over to the high chair. He put a bib around Harper's neck and scooped up some food in the spoon. He touched it to his upper lip.

"I think it's fine," he said, looking at Ravyn for reassurance.

Harper was leaning over the tray with her mouth open, her first few teeth showing, waiting for her dinner.

"She's got teeth!" Bruce exclaimed.

"She does and she may bite down on the spoon. Just gently pull the spoon out if she does."

Bruce fed her spoonful after spoonful of the chunks of peas, carrots, and turkey.

"How will I know she's full?" he asked.

"She'll start spitting out her food or want to take the spoon away from you. She'll want to play, rather than eat."

Bruce gave her another couple of bites before Harper began to try to grab the spoon and ran her hands over the high chair tray, smashing some of the peas that had fallen on the tray.

"I think she's done," Bruce said.

"I think you're right," Ravyn said, unstrapping Harper from the chair. "Let's get your hands washed. Otherwise, you'll have peas in your hair."

Ravyn held Harper by the kitchen sink and rinsed her hands before putting a little soap on them. She dried her daughter's hands and returned her to the high chair. Carol had wiped down the tray and put a sugar cookie on it.

"Should I break this into smaller pieces?" Carol asked.

"Bruce, why don't you give her small bites. I don't think she'll eat it all."

After she'd eaten about half of the cookie, Ravyn got Harper ready for bed. She dressed her in an elf-themed sleeper, then put her down in the portable playpen, in one corner of the dining room. Ravyn hoped she had worn herself out and would sleep. She'd had a big day. Ravyn had had a big day, too. She knew she'd sleep well tonight, too.

As the family was finishing up the Christmas meal, Carol got up from the table. "I hope everyone saved room for dessert. There was a collective groan from the family.

Carol pulled out a pumpkin pie out of the oven and homemade whipped cream. Dessert plates were passed around.

The family continued to talk around the big dining room table. Then Ravyn and Carol cleared the dishes from the table and put up the leftovers.

"Can I send you home with some food?" Carol asked, readying some plastic food containers.

"I'm afraid I can't this year. We're headed to my parents' house first thing tomorrow morning, so it will go to waste. I bet Bruce will take some leftovers. I think he likes his mother's cooking."

"I've got several containers for him. Edward and I can only eat about one more meal and then I'll have to toss it. Edward doesn't really like leftovers."

"Oh gosh. I love leftovers. I think some foods taste better the next day, after all the flavors mix in."

"I agree. But Edward's not a fan."

"Well, I wish we could take some then. But next year we will."

Marc picked up the sleeping Harper and put her in her car seat while Ravyn packed up the portable playpen and gathered the baby bag.

They stood outside the front door and said their goodbyes.

"Well, I'm glad that is over," Marc said as they pulled out of the driveway.

"What's wrong? I thought you were having a good time."

"Then I should win the Oscar for Best Actor. My father was being his usual self, an ass. Bruce was on his best behavior, so that's good."

"Well, I had a lovely time."

"That's because you spent it in the kitchen with my mother. I wish I could have done the same. I'd have had a much better time."

"I'm sorry you and your father didn't get along."

"Don't be sorry. We've never really gotten along. I'm sure nothing will ever change. We are just two very different people."

Chapter 7

Ravyn and Marc fell into bed Christmas night. Ravyn heard her alarm go off the next morning in what seemed like only moments from the time her head hit the pillow.

"Let's hit snooze and sleep in," Marc said. "We have to leave by noon, right?"

"I'll hit snooze, but your daughter may not appreciate it."

"I'll get her if she wakes up."

A half-hour later, Ravyn awoke to hear Harper crying and her husband snoring. She felt like poking Marc in the ribs. Instead, she sighed and got up, padding out to Harper's room.

She found Harper standing up in her crib next to Felix. Ravyn smiled and got her daughter changed into a dry diaper and brought her into the kitchen to her high chair.

Felix followed the pair, weaving between Ravyn's legs and meowing for his food, too.

"Dada?" Harper asked, pointing toward the master bedroom.

"Dada is sleeping, shhh," Ravyn told her daughter, putting her finger to her lips. Harper did the same and made a little hissing sound.

Ravyn put a few pieces of cereal on Harper's high chair tray, then got kibble out for Felix.

"What do you want for breakfast, Harper?" Ravyn asked, turning on the coffee maker and pulling out some unsweetened cereal.

She grabbed a ripe banana and cut it into small pieces. She dropped a few on the tray, then heated up the cereal in the microwave. A little milk cooled the cereal so Ravyn could feed it to Harper.

Harper kept stuffing banana pieces in her mouth. "Slow down," Ravyn said, removing a few pieces of banana. Harper began to pout. "How about some cereal?"

Ravyn got the cereal on the spoon, but Harper was being fussy. She kept her mouth closed.

"Can I help?" Marc asked, coming into the kitchen.

"I thought you were still asleep."

"I was, but I can smell the coffee," he said, pouring himself a cup of the rich dark coffee. He sat down in another chair at the table and took the spoon from Ravyn. "Airplane 123 requests landing, Captain Harper."

Harper immediately opened her mouth as Marc made little swirls and fed her the cereal.

"You have a gift," Ravyn said, standing up. "I'm going to take a quick shower."

"Take your time. We're fine here."

The family was on the road for Easley, South Carolina, where Ravyn's parents lived, shortly before one o'clock. Traffic slowed on northbound Interstate 85 and even more so as they neared its split with Interstate 985, which led to Lake Lanier.

"I wonder why there's so much traffic?" Ravyn asked.

Soon they came to a full stop and crawled along the highway. Ravyn pulled out her phone to see what the trouble was. A solid red line appeared on the Waze traffic map.

"Looks like there is an accident up ahead. I'm not sure Waze will reroute us until we get closer to an exit."

"Hopefully we won't be here too long," Marc said. He looked in the rearview mirror and saw Harper was asleep in her car seat. "Harper's out. Hope she stays that way for a little while."

"It helps to give her a little snack before we travel. She gets sleepy."

The family arrived at Ravyn's parents' house in South Carolina an hour and a half later than they expected. The accident had involved several vehicles and rescue personnel had blocked all lanes of the highway to clear the wreckage.

At one point Marc, along with several other men, had disappeared into the tree line. Ravyn made Marc pull over at the first exit they could so she could get to a gas station restroom as soon as traffic began moving.

Two hours later, they finally arrived at the Shaw house. The smell of turkey filled the house as they entered.

"Smells great in here," Marc said.

"I hope you are hungry," said Kaye Shaw, Ravyn's mother. "I've fixed for an army. Nick, Jane, and Connor are here. We'll eat in about two hours. Now let me see my granddaughter."

Baby Steps

Ravyn handed over Harper, who went willingly to Kaye. Ravyn was glad her daughter was warming up to family members. She went in to see her sister and her family.

"Hey! Sorry we are later than we expected. I'm sure mom told you there was a bad wreck," Ravyn said, giving her sister a hug. She then hugged her brother-in-law and turned her attention to Connor. "How's my sweet boy?"

"He's walking now," Jane said. "Just started. That's why he's got that little bump on his head. He's already taken a header after charging off a small step."

Ravyn rubbed her hand over Connor's forehead. "Poor you. Did you fall down and go boom?"

"Scared me to death. He screamed bloody murder. I called the pediatrician right away, but she didn't think he had a concussion. We just watched him for several hours."

"Harper's not walking just yet. She's crawling and pulling herself up, though. I don't think it will be much longer."

"Where do you want us to put our things?" Marc asked.

"Ravyn's old room, upstairs," Kaye said.

Marc disappeared with their bag and Harper's bag. He'd have to go back to the car for her playpen.

When Marc returned to the house, John, Ravyn's father, called out, "Marc, can I interest you in a cold beer or do you want something stronger?"

"A cold beer would be great. I'll have a scotch later, after dinner."

"Sounds good. A new brewery opened in Greenville a couple of months ago. Jane and Nick brought some of their craft beers, IPAs mostly."

"That sounds great. You know Sweetwater Brewery is in Atlanta. I should have thought to bring some," Marc said.

"Oh, we can get that here," John replied.

John opened a beer bottle and handed it to Marc. Then he opened his. The men clinked their bottle necks.

"Cheers to having our families together," John said.

"I'll drink to that."

The families finished their second Christmas dinner and the adults stayed up late into the night. The infants had been asleep for hours when the adults finally headed to bed.

Ravyn and Marc got into the full bed of Ravyn's youth.

"Guess we're going to have to cuddle tonight," Marc said, rolling over to spoon Ravyn.

"Maybe we need to trade in our king bed for a full," Ravyn teased.

"Not on your life. But for the next couple of days, it will be nice," he replied. "God, I have such a nice time when I'm with your family. Why can't my father be a bit more like yours?"

"I'm glad you get along with my family. They love you."

"I love them, too."

"I think we are going to the Greenville Zoo tomorrow. It opens at 10 a.m. My mother said she'd like to take the children. Both kids will probably sleep through some of it."

"Maybe not. I bet they enjoy it."

"Well, the nice thing is mom will be up early and can help with both kids. We might get to sleep in a bit."

"Heaven," Marc said.

Ravyn could feel his soft breath on her neck as she fell asleep in his arms.

In just three short fun-packed days, Marc, Ravyn, and Harper were packed back in Ravyn's SUV and headed back to Atlanta.

"I'm glad we have the rest of the week off," Marc said.

"Me too. I love my family and yours, but I'm ready to just be home, do laundry, and have some family time of our own," she replied.

"Agreed. I need to hit the gym. It seems all we did since Christmas Eve was eat."

"I think you've pretty well described our adventures. I wouldn't mind a run in the neighborhood either. My jeans feel tight."

"Do you want to make plans for New Year's Eve?"

"Honey, I'm not ready to leave Harper with a sitter just yet," Ravyn said.

"No, I mean we could invite a few neighbors over, have some snacks and drinks, ring in the new year, and kick them out."

Ravyn laughed. "Well, Arthur and Eleanor might come, but Eleanor tells me they are early birds. They might come over, have a drink and fall asleep on our couch."

"We could invite Julie over," Marc suggested.

"I'll ask, but she might not want the girls to stay up that late."

"I just bet her daughters will want to stay up late for New Year's. Whether she wants them to be up is another matter."

"It might be a repeat of Christmas Eve, with all three kids asleep in our guest room while the adults drink and eat."

"That's not so bad, is it?"

"Not for us. We're not leaving the house. Julie might not want to be on the roads so late on a night when other folks are overdoing it."

"Then see if some neighbors can come. They can walk home."

"OK. I'll see if Arthur and Eleanor can come, and Delaine and Doug might come if they don't have plans."

"He's the city planner, right?"

"Yes. She works for a company in Gainesville."

"Gainesville? That's a long commute."

"She says it's not too bad. She's going against traffic."

"Well, maybe they'll come. If not, it will just be you and me to party all night."

"I bet you and I are in bed long before midnight, Marc."

"Somehow, I think you are right. Maybe we don't need to invite anyone over."

"Maybe not," Ravyn agreed. She honestly thought a quiet evening to themselves was just what they needed.

On New Year's Eve, Marc and Ravyn sat on the couch in front of the fireplace and could barely stay awake to see the New York City ball drop to ring in 2018. They managed to make it to midnight and watched the countdown on TV.

"Happy New Year, Marc," Ravyn said, kissing her husband.

"Happy New Year, my darling. May 2018 be our best year yet."

"I want to start the year right. Let's make love."

"Your wish is my command," Marc said.

Ravyn began to undress in the bedroom, but Marc made her stop.

"I want you to undress slowly," he said.

"Like a striptease?"

"Not like a striptease, just slowly. I want to enjoy your body. And I wouldn't mind a little dirty talk." He grinned.

But Ravyn frowned. "My body isn't young and perky anymore."

"What are you talking about?"

"I haven't lost my baby weight. My belly is pouchy."

"What?"

"I have a baby belly. A jelly belly."

"Ravyn, I love you. I love your baby belly. That jelly belly, as you call it, created our daughter," Marc said, choking up and hugging her close, the striptease he requested forgotten for the moment.

"Marc, that is so sweet," Ravyn replied, starting to cry.

"Hey, we can't be sad. New Year's is supposed to be happy. You know, Happy New Year!"

Ravyn laughed through her tears. "This is why I love you."

"It's why I love you more. Now take your clothes off slowly," he said, thinking about her getting naked. "My dick is getting hard."

"Now that's my kind of talk. Dirty talk, too."

Ravyn and Marc made love and fell asleep in each other's arms. As she drifted off to sleep, Ravyn felt better about her naked body. She'd been worried since she'd seen her body change. That she wasn't as attractive to Marc as she used to be. That Laura Lucas's gift had been prophetic. Motherhood was harder than she thought.

Harper sounded her alarm that she was hungry far earlier than Marc and Ravyn were ready. Marc threw his arm across his face. It wasn't even daybreak yet.

Ravyn almost wished they were back at her parents' house, where her mother took Harper and Connor and let the new parents sleep in.

"I'll get her," Marc said, groping for his pajama bottoms in the dark.

"Thank you," Ravyn said, sleepily. "I'll be up in a minute."

"Go back to sleep," Marc whispered.

Ravyn slept for another two hours, then dragged herself out of the warm bed. She found Marc sitting in the living room, reading Atlanta's daily newspaper – the newspaper she used to work for – with Harper sleeping in her playpen.

Marc had started a fire in the fireplace since Atlanta's mornings had turned cold again.

"Good morning, beautiful," he said as Ravyn reached for the coffee before coming to join him on the couch.

"Good morning, lover. Thanks for taking Harper watch this morning. I'll get up with her tomorrow so you can sleep in. Is it wrong I wished we were back at my parents' house and my mom would take Harper for us?"

"That was nice of her. Can she come live with us and be our nanny full time?"

"Be careful what you wish for! She might take you up on that. But she'd miss Connor, too. Well, and my dad. What are we doing today? Are you heading to the gym?"

"I'd like to. May I?"

"Of course. I'll wait until it warms up a little to go for a run, so I'll go when you come back. I'm kind of sad I didn't sign up for the Resolution Run this year."

"Why didn't you? I could have watched Harper."

"I wasn't sure I would be ready to run just yet. Next year I'll sign up for it."

The pair traded off workouts and, in the evening, had a quiet meal at the smaller breakfast table, feeding Harper before putting her to bed.

They cuddled on the couch in front of a fire while they watched a movie on TV, then headed to bed.

As they cuddled after making love, Ravyn asked Marc, "Have you thought about what we're going to do for Harper's first birthday?"

"That's a month away," he said, yawning.

"Well, I want to plan something small. Maybe just our families on the Sunday after her birthday. Her birthday is on a Saturday. I think we should celebrate with just us on Saturday. Everyone else can come Sunday. Or maybe we could celebrate Friday and have the families come Saturday. They'd probably want to do that instead."

"Sounds good," Marc said, rolling over on his side and falling asleep.

Ravyn wasn't sure he'd remember agreeing to her idea in the morning, but she was glad she was thinking about the birthday. She wanted to let everyone know so they could plan to come.

She fell asleep thinking of what she'd serve for lunch and making a grocery list in her head.

Marc's cell phone went off in the middle of the night. Normally, he had his phone on Do Not Disturb, but he allowed his contacts to ring through. His mother was calling.

"Hello?" he asked. "What's wrong, Mom?"

"It's your father," Carol said.

Marc could hear the distress in her voice. "What's wrong?"

Ravyn sat up, alerted to Marc's panicked voice.

"He's had a heart attack. I'm at Northside Hospital."

"I'm on my way," Marc said, sitting up and reaching for the bedside light.

"What's happening? What's the matter?" Ravyn asked.

"My father had a heart attack. He's at Northside. I've gotta go. My mom sounds really bad."

"Oh, God, Marc!"

"I know," he said, getting dressed quickly and throwing on a heavy sweater.

Ravyn got up and put on her robe. "Do you want some coffee to go?"

"No. I don't have time. I've just gotta get up there."

"Of course. Let me know how he is as soon as you know."

"I will," Marc said as he stood at the front door. "I love you."

"I love you, too."

Marc kissed her deeply, then disappeared into the dark. Ravyn stood at the front door, the frigid air making her feet feel cold. Marc started his older BMW, switched on the headlights, and pulled out of their short driveway. Ravyn waved from the door, before returning to the warm house.

Ravyn had a hard time falling back to sleep. She slept fitfully, waking to bad dreams.

She finally just got up around five in the morning. She knew Harper would also be up soon.

She texted Marc asking if there was any news.

He replied his father was in ICU and was critical. He'd suffered a major heart attack. But he was still alive.

That was good news, Ravyn thought.

Marc relayed his mother wasn't doing so well, though. He would probably go back to the Dunwoody house to look after her. Was Ravyn OK to look after Harper alone today? he asked.

Ravyn assured him they would be fine but hoped his father would recover and Marc would be home later that night.

But Marc didn't return that night. He stayed at his parent's Dunwoody home with his mother. Ravyn thought surely he would have come home for a change of clothes.

The next day, Marc said he and his mother were headed back to the hospital. Ravyn asked if she and Harper should go up to the hospital.

Marc said not to come. Harper wouldn't be allowed in the hospital, and certainly not in the ICU.

Was there anything she could bring them?

Marc said if she could bring some lunch, that would be great. She should text when she got to the hospital, and he'd come out to get the lunch she brought.

Ravyn packed Harper into her car seat and drove to Publix to get some sub sandwiches for Marc and Carol. She'd texted them, asking what they wanted and put in the order at the deli. She grabbed some snacks, soft drinks, and a couple of apples, too, before checking out.

When she arrived at the Northside Hospital parking lot, she texted Marc, who came out for the sandwiches. She also handed him a duffel bag with some clothes, including underwear, khakis, and a dress shirt for work. She wasn't sure he was coming home that Sunday night, either.

"I'm sorry," Marc said as he reached through the driver's window to kiss his wife. "Dad's not doing well. I might not be home tonight. Thanks for the clothes."

"Please give your mother our love. I'm sorry your father is so ill."

Marc looked pained. "I'll give my mother your love. It's just… my father. I should have…"

Marc got choked up on the words.

Ravyn reached her hand through the open window and touched Marc's cheek. "He knows you love him."

"I don't think he does, Ravyn. Because I never told him."

"When he gets well you can tell him."

"I just hope so. I just…"

"I know. I know you love him."

Baby Steps

Marc bent his head through the driver's window and kissed Ravyn deeply. "I love you."

"I love you, too."

Ravyn drove away from the hospital with a terrible feeling in the pit of her stomach.

She got home, got Harper into the house, and got her fed. They played with some wooden blocks, then Ravyn put Harper down for an afternoon nap. Harper didn't sleep all that long. At least that's what Ravyn thought when Harper awoke Ravyn from her nap.

Ravyn texted Marc, asking if he was coming home that day.

Marc replied he was still at the hospital with his mother and then would likely go back to the Dunwoody house and go to work from there on Monday. He missed her, she said.

Ravyn was disappointed Marc was not coming home, but she told him she understood. Had Marc talked to Bruce? How was he handling the news?

Marc said he had not been able to reach Bruce, even though his brother worked at Northside Hospital. He'd texted him about their father's heart attack, but neither he nor his mother had seen Bruce. He had not come to the ICU to see their father.

Ravyn thought that was odd. She worried about Bruce. Why hadn't he gone to see his father?

Next, Ravyn texted Bruce asking if he was OK. Had he seen his father? Did he know Marc and his mother were trying to reach him? She didn't get a response.

Ravyn had just put Harper to bed after reading her "Goodnight Moon" for what felt like the hundredth time when Marc called.

"Marc? How's your father?"

Marc was silent, then croaked, "He's dead."

"What?" Ravyn asked, alarmed.

"He's dead, Ravyn. He never recovered. He never regained consciousness. He's gone." Marc began to cry.

"Marc, Marc, I'm so sorry." Now Ravyn was crying too. She hadn't necessarily gotten along with her father-in-law, but she never wished him any harm.

"Mother's not doing well. I'm going home with her. I'll stay with her overnight."

"Marc, please come home. Please."

"I can't," he choked. "I've got to be with my mother. She needs me."

"Marc, we need you. Please come home."

"I can't."

Ravyn hung up with Marc, heartbroken. She just wanted to hold him tonight. She wanted to ease his broken heart. She wanted to make love to him tenderly to show him how much she loved him.

Ravyn tossed and turned in her marital bed, missing Marc next to her.

Marc drove his mother home. The doctor had prescribed some sleeping pills for his mother so she could sleep that night. Marc had picked up the script on the way out of the hospital. His mother was devastated. Marc thought she looked catatonic. She barely spoke after she learned her husband of 45 years had died.

Marc felt he could not leave her alone. He'd called his sister Brooke to let her know their father had died. He had talked to her briefly. He knew she was shocked. He'd also tried to reach his brother Bruce but was only able to leave a voicemail. He was worried about Bruce. Worried that he was drinking or using drugs again.

Marc got his mother into the house, made sure she took her sleeping pill with some water, then climbed the stairs to his childhood bedroom.

Marc then broke down sobbing. He regretted he'd never gotten the chance to talk to his father after the heart attack. He regretted he'd never get the chance to tell him he loved him. He was confused about his emotions.

Marc was angry, then sad, then felt devoid of emotion. Then he was angry and sad again.

He slept poorly, wishing he could hold Ravyn in his arms. But he didn't want her to see him cry.

Chapter 8

Ravyn tried to be understanding about Marc's absence. On Friday morning, the day after her father-in-law died, she got Harper to daycare before heading to her own work downtown. That evening, Ravyn then picked her up.

Marc normally took Harper to daycare and Ravyn noticed her daughter was confused with the schedule change.

Marc continued to call Ravyn every evening and make excuses why he couldn't come home.

Ravyn was frustrated. She wanted her husband home. She wanted to comfort him. She wanted him to see his daughter. Ravyn tried to explain Harper was asking for her dada and where he was. She tried to tell him Harper needed him. That Ravyn needed him.

In bed at night, Ravyn felt the sexual frustration of not having Marc near her. Not having him make love to her. Her frustration turned into anger.

"Why aren't you coming home?" Ravyn pleaded with Marc.

"My mother needs me," he replied.

"Your daughter needs you. I need you," she responded, angry. "I know you want to be there for your mother, but your family needs you, too. I don't understand why you aren't here."

"I'm sorry. I'm sorry. My mother isn't doing well. And we're trying to plan the funeral."

"When is the funeral?"

"Tuesday."

"Will you be home before the funeral at least?"

"Probably not. I'm sorry. My mother is so distraught."

"OK," Ravyn said, trying to keep the anger out of her voice. "Let me know the details of the funeral. We will be there. We love you, Marc."

"I love you, too, Ravyn. I'll be home soon."

Ravyn hung up with Marc but wasn't sure he was being truthful. Why hadn't he come home?

Marc finally came home Monday evening. Harper was excited to see her daddy. She kept pointing at him, saying, "Dada."

"Dada's home, sweet pea," he said, picking Harper up.

"She missed you," Ravyn said.

"I missed her. And I missed you," he replied.

"How is your mother?"

"She's still upset. She went to see her doctor today. He prescribed an antidepressant and some more sleeping pills. She wasn't sleeping at all. She just walked around the house at night. She had a sleeping pill the first night, and it worked that night. Then she couldn't sleep after that, even when she took the sleeping pills, and just walked around like a zombie. I'm worried about her."

"I'm sorry she's suffering."

"I hope the medication helps. The funeral is tomorrow afternoon. Visitation is a half hour before that. Brooke arrived last night. We stayed up and talked about the funeral, what we're going to say during the service. We don't know where Bruce is. He hasn't shown up at work, either. He'll be fired if he doesn't show up or call in. I talked to his supervisor today and told her that his father died. She put him down for bereavement leave, but he needs to call in."

"I tried calling him, too, but I haven't heard from him."

"I'm guessing he's drinking again. He just can't do anything right."

"Marc, he lost his father, too."

"That's no excuse," Marc said bitterly. "I lost my father and I'm not out drunk or using drugs."

"We don't know he's doing that, Marc."

"Stop defending him. I'd bet money he is. I doubt he shows up for the funeral, and if he does, he damn well better show up sober. My mother has been through enough."

"Do you need me to press your dark suit?" Ravyn asked, changing the subject.

"I'll wear my charcoal suit. I think it's still pressed from the last time it was dry cleaned."

"OK. I've got a navy dress I can put on Harper."

"Our family will be seated in the first two rows of the funeral home's chapel."

"No church?"

"My father was not religious. The funeral home chapel is the best choice. The reading of the will is Friday," Marc said softly.

"Where?"

"At my father's law office. He had another attorney in his office draw it up."

"Should I go with you?"

"Would you?"

"Of course I will."

Just then Marc's cell phone rang. It was his sister Brooke. She said they finally heard from Bruce.

"How did he sound? Drunk?"

Brooke said she couldn't tell, but that he would be at the funeral Tuesday, and Friday at the reading of the will. He said he'd also called his supervisor at work. Brooke said she was relieved he hadn't been fired.

Marc told his sister he was surprised that their brother hadn't been.

"I think his supervisor was sympathetic that his father — our father — had died," she said.

"I just can't believe him. Our mother needs her family with her now and he's been MIA."

"Marc, why are you so angry at him? His father has died, too."

"I'm angry because he's such a fuck up, Brooke!"

"You're angry because your little brother has had a harder life than you, and you hold it against him."

"Had a harder life than me? What are you talking about?"

Brooke was silent for a moment, then said softly, "You know he was sexually assaulted as a boy, don't you?"

"What!? What are you talking about? I don't believe it."

"A camp counselor messed with him."

"What do you mean messed with him?"

"Bullied him and then sexually assaulted him. He told me about it."

"He told you and not me?"

"Given your reaction to the news, I'm not surprised at all he didn't tell you. You're not exactly empathetic."

"When did he tell you?"

"Several years ago. He was 14 or 15 when it happened. He didn't tell me until he was 35 or so when he got out of rehab."

"Which rehab?" Marc scoffed. "Did Mom and Dad know?"

"Mom did. He told her. I don't think he ever told Dad. I don't think he ever could tell Dad."

"Well, I'm sorry he couldn't confide in me, either. I guess it lets me know he puts me in Dad's category."

"Don't be that way, Marc. I'm sure he didn't tell you because you are so judgmental. He needs some understanding, not judgment."

"I'm judgmental?!" Marc asked, angry. "Is that what you think of me?"

"Listen, I'm not going to have an argument with you over the phone. I love you, you know that. But you need to cut Bruce a little slack. The assault really affected him. He was a teenager, Marc. A half-grown man, really. You are a father now. You'd kill anyone who harmed Harper."

Marc didn't say anything, then tightly said, "I'd kill any son of a bitch who lays a finger on my daughter."

"Exactly. Bruce is still hurting, Marc. You don't just bounce back from that."

"OK. I'll cut him some slack."

"Don't just say it, Marc. Do it."

"OK, OK. I'll see you tomorrow at the visitation and funeral. Then I'll be ready for a scotch."

"Mom says she's going to have people over to the house after the service. Bring your flask."

Marc worked hard to keep his emotions in check during the memorial service. He was stoic during the visitation, as well, but during the memorial service, he kept having to clear his throat. Brooke kept dabbing her eyes with a tissue and put her arm around her mother, who sobbed during the ceremony.

Marc had seen Bruce's bloodshot eyes when he arrived for the service. He felt sure his brother was drunk. During the ceremony, Marc looked over to see his brother Bruce overcome with emotion. Carol took Bruce's hand halfway through the funeral and wouldn't let go.

Ravyn held Marc's hand throughout the eulogy. She was grateful Harper was quiet and not squirming in Ravyn's lap. Harper did begin to babble during the quiet of the service, and Ravyn started to get up to take her to the back of the chapel, but Marc pulled her back down to her seat. "Let her be," he whispered. "She's fine."

When the service was over, the family moved to the doors, as mourners began to walk up the aisle and offer their condolences. Most were members of his father's law firm. A few were neighbors or his mother's friends.

Marc glanced at his mother and noticed how tired she looked. Suddenly it struck Marc how old she now looked, too. It seemed to him, his mother, who was in her early 60s, had aged a decade since her husband's death not even a week ago.

Marc was anxious to get back to the house. He knew some people would come back to the Dunwoody house with them to pay their respects, but he just wanted to take off his funeral clothes and be alone with his immediate family.

Marc walked up the front steps to his childhood home but could hear someone vomiting near the side of the house. He walked around and found Bruce kneeling and being sick in the bushes.

"Bruce," Marc said.

"Leave me alone," Bruce hoarsely whispered, turning his face from his brother.

"Let me go get you a towel," Marc said.

"Leave me alone. I don't need your help," Bruce replied. But as he stood up, he lost his balance and fell, rolling slightly downhill in the grass.

"I think you do," Marc said, putting his hand out to help his brother to his feet.

"I don't need you," Bruce spat.

"Well, our mother does need you, so pull yourself together, Bruce," Marc said, getting angry. "She needs us to be strong for her. Can't you see she's a wreck?"

Brooke could hear raised voices and came around the house to find Marc and Bruce.

"What is going on? People can hear you," she hissed.

"Bruce needs a towel to freshen up a bit. He lost his balance and fell," Marc replied, trying to cover for his brother. "I was just going to get one for him."

Marc walked briskly to the side door and into the kitchen, pulling a kitchen towel out of the drawer, filling a glass with water, and returning to where Bruce and Brooke were standing.

"Here," he said, handing the water glass and the towel to Bruce.

Bruce took both without a word, guzzled half the water, then wiped his mouth before getting a mouthful of water and spitting it out on the ground. He then wiped his mouth again.

"You're going to be OK, Bruce," Brooke said, rubbing her younger brother's arm. "Come into the house."

Brooke led Bruce to the side entrance of the house. Marc went back to the front of the house and through the front door. Mourners and neighbors expressed their condolences, shaking Marc's hand and gripping him by the shoulder.

"He was so young."

"I never expected it."

"How is your mother holding up?"

"Let us know if we can do anything."

"Is there an interment ceremony?"

Marc heard the questions but could only nod politely or give short answers. The family had decided to have their father cremated and would decide what to do with the urn later. When the last of the mourners left, Marc collapsed on the sofa, exhausted.

Ravyn came over and sat beside him, putting her hand on his leg. "Are you OK?"

Marc shook his head no.

"Can I get you a scotch?"

"Yeah. Make it a double."

Ravyn stood up and went to the wet bar in the corner of the living room, pulling down a crystal low ball glass and filling it with a few pieces of ice from the icemaker under the countertop and then filling the glass with a generous portion of scotch. She returned and placed it in his outstretched hand.

"Thanks," he murmured, taking a long sip. "Where's Harper?"

"Upstairs taking a nap in your bedroom."

"Is she on the bed?"

"No. I packed her playpen. She's sleeping in that."

"You should have told me. I'd have brought it in."

"Your sister helped me."

"Where's Bruce?"

"I haven't seen him in a while. I don't think he was feeling very well."

"He was drunk."

"He was overcome with grief. I think he took an Uber home."

"I should hope so. I don't think he was in any condition to drive."

"I think your sister insisted he take Uber. I think she hid his keys."

"Glad she has brains in this family."

"I'm worried about you. You look tired. Why don't we go home soon?"

"I am tired. I want to stay just a bit longer to make sure my mother is OK. Why don't you and Harper go home, though. No need for you both to stay here. It's been a tiring day."

Ravyn's brow wrinkled. "Promise me you are coming home tonight."

"Why wouldn't I?"

"Don't sit here all night, brood and drink scotch, OK?"

Marc looked at Ravyn in disbelief. "Are you saying I drink too much?"

"I'm saying you've had a long, emotional day. You can get in one of your moods and sip on that scotch all night."

"Nice to know my wife has my back," he said, his face darkening.

"I do have your back, Marc. I'd like you to come home and be with your family, too," Ravyn pleaded. "We are here for you as well."

"I'll see you when I get home," he said gruffly. Marc stood up and walked out of the living room.

Ravyn got home with Harper, got her fed, and fell asleep on the leather couch with Harper in her playpen. Ravyn awoke with a start and realized it was dark outside. Marc was still not home.

She reached for her phone to see if he had called or texted her. There were no messages. She texted him but got no response.

Ravyn sighed. She didn't expect her husband to come home that night.

Baby Steps

Ravyn heard the lock being opened to the front door and reached for her phone to check the time. Her phone read five in the morning.

She grabbed her robe and padded out to the living room. Marc had lain down on the couch and pulled a lap blanket over him.

"Aren't you coming to bed?" she asked.

"I didn't want to wake you."

"I heard the door."

"Sorry."

"Come to bed, Marc."

Marc got up, tossed the small blanket on the end of the couch, and followed Ravyn into their bedroom. He undressed quietly.

Ravyn got back into bed and wondered why her husband was acting strangely. "What's the matter?" she asked quietly as he got into bed beside her.

"I'm just tired. Yesterday was a hard day."

"I understand." Ravyn rolled over and wrapped her arms around Marc. She waited to hear his soft snoring, but she never heard it before she fell back asleep.

Ravyn awoke to a silent house. The space next to her, where Marc should have been, was cold and empty. "Marc?" She called out softly. She got up and went into Harper's bedroom. She wasn't in her crib. Alarmed, Ravyn called out more loudly. "Marc! Harper?"

She finally saw the note by the coffeemaker that Marc had taken Harper for a walk in the stroller. Ravyn peeked at the outside thermometer. It read 55 degrees. She hoped Marc had bundled Harper up. She didn't want to have to deal with another cold where she couldn't drop Harper off at daycare.

Ravyn could certainly go to work feeling like death, but her daughter could not. The daycare had a strict policy about when children could not attend.

Ravyn fixed her coffee and sat at the small breakfast table, finally calming down to enjoy the quiet morning. Felix came out of Harper's room and chirped hello, rubbing his big gray head against Ravyn's leg.

"I suppose you'd like your breakfast too, big guy," she said. She stood up and pulled down his kibble, filling his food bowl before refilling his water dish.

Felix buried his face in his food bowl and Ravyn sat back down to her coffee. Just a few minutes later Ravyn heard the back door open. Marc pulled the stroller through the door and motioned to Ravyn that Harper was asleep.

Ravyn stood up and kissed Marc. "I was worried when I couldn't find you."

"I left you a note."

"I found that, but not before I panicked at an all-too-quiet house. And then Harper wasn't in her crib."

"I didn't want to wake you up. You were sleeping pretty soundly."

"How did you sleep?"

Marc shook his head. "I didn't. I got up early, fed Harper, and decided to go for a walk. I thought the crisp air would clear my head."

Ravyn put her hand on Marc's arm and gave it a small squeeze. "Maybe you can take a nap today."

Marc shook his head again. "I'm headed back to my parent's — I mean my mother's — house."

"But you need your rest."

"I can try to nap there if I need to."

"You do need to, Marc. You look like you haven't slept well. Your eyes, I can see it in your eyes."

Ravyn touched Marc's face, putting her palm against his cheek, caressing it. "Come back to bed. Harper's asleep and I'll get her if she wakes up. Come back to bed and rest. You need sleep."

Marc stood up from the breakfast table. "I can't. I'm going to shower and go."

"Let me at least fix you some breakfast."

"I'm not that hungry."

"Marc, let me take care of you."

"I'm not a child, Ravyn. I don't need you to take care of me."

Ravyn looked at Marc stunned. "I'm not saying you are a child. But your father just died. You need some tender loving care, and you are pushing me away."

"I'm not pushing you away, Ravyn," Marc responded louder than he intended. "I'm just trying to look after my mother and be a good son. God knows Bruce can't be one or look after her."

Marc strode into the bedroom and shut the door. He'd never shut the bedroom door on Ravyn. But he couldn't see the hurt in her eyes. He knew he was being an ass, but he couldn't seem to help himself. He felt so alone. Like he was drowning and there was no one to help.

He got into the shower and turned on the water, letting the shower walls get good and steamy before he began to cry.

Marc kissed Ravyn on the cheek as he left the house and gave Harper a little rub under her chin. Ravyn was holding Harper on her hip and Harper reached out for Marc saying "Dada."

"Bye-bye, Harper," Marc said, waving to his daughter. He had a fake smile on his face, but Harper looked at her father and frowned.

Harper's bottom lip quivered and then she began to cry. Harper screeched and tried reaching out to Marc, but Ravyn held on tight, not wanting her daughter to fall to the ground.

"Dada will be back, honey," Ravyn said, smoothing her hand over Harper's forehead and then wiping away her tears. She closed the front door before Marc could see her tears, too.

Ravyn quickly showered and got ready for work. Despite her father-in-law's death, she didn't take any bereavement leave. She got Harper dressed and to daycare and then herself to work, only a few minutes late.

At home after work, Ravyn got the jogging stroller out. The temperature had moderated a bit. She still bundled Harper into her coat and heavier leggings before strapping her in. Ravyn on the other hand wore capris and a long-sleeved athletic shirt. She tied a windbreaker around her waist. Once she started running, she doubted she'd even stop to put it on.

She stepped out onto the neighborhood streets and ran at a quick pace. Not as fast as before the baby. She wanted to run until her legs ached. Ravyn was running off frustration and anger.

She tried not to think about Marc and his bad behavior. She tried to keep her mind blank, just enjoying the sunshine and blue skies today.

When Ravyn got back to the house her legs ached and she was winded. She'd run hard. It felt good to run that hard again. Ravyn knew she'd likely pay for her hard work out with sore muscles tomorrow.

For now, she got the jogging stroller back in the house, unhooked Harper from it, and stood at the refrigerator door filling a glass from the automatic water dispenser.

Ravyn had hoped Harper might have fallen asleep during the run, but she was wide awake.

"Ok, sweetie. Let's get you fed and then it's bed time."

An hour later Ravyn was putting Harper in her crib and softly closed the door. She brought the baby monitor into the bathroom and drew a hot bath, putting in some Epsom salts and a shake of peppermint essential oil.

Ravyn nearly fell asleep herself in the relaxing bath but as the water cooled, she got out, toweled off and put on her sweatpants and sweatshirt.

She fixed herself a light supper before checking on Harper. Then she called Julie to get her caught up. Rayvn just needed a little moral support as well.

"Is this a bad time to talk?"

"No, the girls are over at their father's house with his whore. He's taking them to school tomorrow."

"It's not his regular night to have them, is it?"

"No, but he wanted to change the day."

"I'm calling to complain about my husband, too"

"What's he done now?"

Ravyn recounted Marc's distance and remoteness since his father's death. She was beginning to resent having to care for Harper by herself.

"He told me he wanted to be a team and a real father, but I see him acting more like his own father, I'm sorry to say."

"Are you sure it's not grief? He could be acting this way because he's not dealing well with the death of his father," Julie said.

"Maybe, but I wish he'd talk to me or confide in me. Instead, it feels like he's shutting me out."

"I'm sorry, Ravyn. I know this is difficult for him and for you."

"Thanks for just letting me get it off my chest."

"Any time. You've let me bitch and moan about my husband for several months now. I'm glad I could return the favor."

As the time neared 9:30, Ravyn considered calling Marc, then put her phone down. Dammit, if he didn't care enough to let her know what time he'd be home, she wouldn't call either. She poured herself a large glass of red wine.

Chapter 9

Ravyn hadn't expected Marc would come home that night, but she was still disappointed she'd been right. She was not enjoying the life of a single mother.

She wondered whether to call in a personal day at work to go to the reading of her father-in-law's will. Marc had said it would be at Edward's law firm. She called into her office and said she'd be working from home but dropped Harper off at daycare. Ravyn would get a lot more work done without her daughter in the house.

Then she would wait until she heard from Marc.

By noon she decided to text him to see what time she needed to be there.

Sorry, I should have called you earlier. It's at two this afternoon. I'll meet you in the lobby of the building at 1:30, he replied.

Yes, you should have called me last night and you should have come home, she wanted to reply. Instead, she just texted him she'd be there at 1:30.

Ravyn said she'd have to get Harper from daycare right after the reading of the will.

Thanks, was Marc's response.

Ravyn once again felt angry at her husband. He could have offered to get Harper. The law office was in Midtown after all — right across from the daycare.

Ravyn wore her black skirt and the teal sweater Marc had gotten her several Christmases ago when they were still dating. She hoped he appreciated the gesture.

When she got to the lobby, she saw Marc pacing in front of the security desk. Ravyn showed her ID and got a visitor's badge before Marc led her to the bank of elevators.

"Brooke's already here. Bruce said he was coming but he hasn't shown up yet. Mother's here as well."

"How are you doing?" she asked, putting her hand on his back.

Ravyn could feel him tense up. "I'm fine."

"You don't seem fine. You look exhausted."

"I'm fine. Really." He gave Ravyn a weak smile before the elevator door opened and they stepped out into a well-appointed law firm lobby.

The receptionist pointed down the hall, but Marc was already steering Ravyn to the office marked James Smith Jr.

Smith was a gray-haired man with thinning hair and a comb-over. He shook Ravyn's hand and said he was sorry they had to meet this way. Ravyn thought she had met him at the funeral but there were so many people she didn't know that day, so she wasn't sure.

They made small talk until about two o'clock when the front desk receptionist buzzed that Bruce Linder had arrived. Smith sent his assistant to guide Bruce to the office.

If Ravyn thought Marc looked exhausted, Bruce looked worse. His eyes were bloodshot and glassy. Marc stiffened at the sight of his brother, but Carol hugged her youngest son and sat him down next to her.

Smith explained why they were all gathered. He said this was the final will of Edward Linder. He prefaced by saying he knew there were things in the will that would be upsetting or cause distress. That he had tried to talk Edward out of creating such a will.

Marc looked at his mother, who looked stricken, her lips pressed together.

Smith talked to Brooke first, saying she would be given an inheritance and a trust would be set up for her children. Brooke nodded, dabbing her eyes with a tissue.

Smith then turned to Marc, saying his father didn't leave him an inheritance but canceled the debt owed to Edward and his estate. Marc frowned at this news but then nodded.

The remainder of the inheritance would go to Carol, his wife, Smith said.

"What about Bruce?" Carol asked.

Smith looked pained and frowned. "I'm sorry, Mrs. Linder, Carol. Edward disinherited Bruce. He gets no money from the estate."

"Oh!" Carol cried out.

Bruce looked stunned, then angry. Bruce jumped from the office sofa and bolted out the door.

"Bruce!" Carol called out. "Bruce!"

"I'll get him," Marc said. Marc stood up to go after Bruce, but when he entered the hallway, Bruce wasn't there.

"Did you see where my brother went?" he asked Smith's assistant, who was seated at her desk.

"He ran out into the lobby area," she said, pointing. "I saw him push the button for the elevator. He just got on. You just missed him. Is everything OK? He seemed, ah, distressed."

"He just got some bad news. Let me see if I can catch up with him."

Marc pushed the elevator's down button and waited for the car to arrive. By the time Marc got to the office's main lobby, Bruce was nowhere to be seen.

Marc sighed and got back on the elevator, returning to Smith's office.

"Did you catch him?" Carol asked.

"He's gone. I'm not sure where he went."

"You've got to find him. His father just can't..." Carol began to cry.

"Mom, we'll find him," Brooke said, hugging her mother.

"Tell him I'll give him the inheritance his father wouldn't. It will be my money now. I'll take care of him."

Marc said nothing but was angry that his mother was willing to part with some of her inheritance for Bruce, but not him.

Ravyn gave Marc a worried look. She could tell he was upset by the turn of events in the will. Wasn't the clearing of the debt owed to Edward kind of an inheritance? She knew Marc had taken a second mortgage out on his house to pay his father back the hundreds of thousands he had borrowed to keep LindMark Enterprises afloat.

When Black Kat Investors had purchased a majority stake in Marc's company, it meant Marc could pay his father back most of the debt, but not all of it. The $3 million Black Kat had paid Marc wasn't really $3 million in the end. It paid off part of the debt to Edward Linder, who had charged Marc interest on the money Marc had borrowed. She and Marc were still paying off the second mortgage.

The reading of the will was over and the family left feeling worse than when they came into the office.

"I'm sorry for your loss," James Smith said. "And I'm sorry I couldn't talk Edward out of this final will. I tried to counsel him that this would create discord in the family. He was a stubborn man and a hell of a lawyer."

Smith took off his glasses, wiped his eyes, and put his glasses back on. "And a hell of a good friend," he said, huskily.

He showed the family to the door and walked them to the elevator bank. The family got into the car and rode down to the lobby in silence.

Ravyn took Marc's hand as they rode down. "I'll meet you back at the house," she said to him in the lobby.

"I'm going to head over to my mother's house first."

Ravyn frowned. "Please come home tonight," she pleaded.

"We'll discuss this later," Marc said curtly.

Ravyn got in her Honda CRV and drove across the street to pick up Harper. She knew she'd be alone again that night.

Ravyn's cell phone rang about ten o'clock that evening. She was surprised it was Bruce.

"Bruce? Where are you? We were all worried when you left today. Are you OK?"

"Ravyn, I need your help. I've been arrested."

"Arrested?"

"For DUI — driving under the influence."

"I know what it means."

"They've impounded my car," Bruce started to cry. "Blaze is at my apartment. I can't go get him. Can you get him? Please, Ravyn. I can't lose Blaze too."

"OK, but I don't have your key. Who has your spare key?"

"My landlord should let you in."

Bruce gave Ravyn the number for his landlord and Ravyn agreed to call him and to go get Blaze.

Ravyn sighed. She'd have to wake Harper up to go get Blaze. She had no idea how Blaze and Felix would get along and she had no idea what Marc would say to Blaze being in the house. She knew Marc wasn't all that wild about Felix in the house. She could imagine what he'd think about a dog in the house, especially Bruce's dog.

Ravyn pulled up to Bruce's apartment building. It was a two-story building with outside stairs and a breezeway to each apartment.

Bruce's landlord let Ravyn into Bruce's apartment and Ravyn was shocked at its contents. She could smell old takeout food and could tell Blaze had had accidents in this apartment.

The small studio apartment had no furniture except for a mattress on the floor, a single chair, a TV tray, and a small TV stand with an old TV on it. She didn't see any cable, so she assumed he used rabbit ears to get any TV signal.

Why hadn't Bruce asked her for any furniture? She had half of her old furniture still stored in Marc's garage. She could have given him some things. She'd had no idea he lived in squalor, really.

Her furniture was in Marc's garage because a mouse infestation at her storage unit meant most of her things were ruined. But not everything. Why hadn't Bruce asked for anything?

Blaze stood in the center of what Ravyn assumed was the living room but was hesitant to come forward. Ravyn shifted a sleepy Harper on her hip and softly called to Blaze.

"Come here, boy," she cajoled. "Let's go for a ride."

She looked around for a leash. She had not come prepared to collect a dog. She didn't have a crate. Blaze did have a collar, but she couldn't carry both Blaze and Harper to her car.

"Do you see a leash?" Ravyn asked the landlord. He pointed to the countertop. Ravyn grabbed what she thought was a leash, but it was really a rope with a clip on it.

"Let's go for a ride, Blaze," she said softly again.

"You know I shouldn't even have let you in," the landlord said. "Bruce owes me last month's rent."

"Well, I don't have any money on me right now," she said, skeptical that the landlord was trying to take advantage of her good nature. "Can I call you tomorrow? I have my daughter with me, and I'll have this dog. I've got my hands full tonight. Can you help me carry the dog food down to my car?"

"It will cost you $10," the landlord said.

"Seriously? You are going to charge me to carry the dog food down to the car?" Ravyn asked, angry. "Forget it. I can see you are not a kind man."

The landlord shrugged his shoulders.

Ravyn reluctantly put Harper down on the mattress and grabbed some of the takeout boxes to throw in the kitchen trash bin. When she opened the lid, she could see empty beer bottles and cans and a couple of empty liquor bottles.

Ravyn frowned at the sight. She put the leash on Blaze after some more cajoling, picked up Harper, then grabbed the bag of dog food in the same hand she had the leash. She stomped down the stairs to her car.

She dropped the dog food on the ground, opened the back passenger door, and put Harper in her car seat. Blaze jumped in the back and laid down on the seat next to Harper. Ravyn then put the dog food on the floorboard and shut the door. She walked briskly to the driver's door and got in.

Ravyn did not even acknowledge the landlord. She thought he was a skeevy asshole. She just wanted out of the complex and back to her Buckhead home.

Ravyn pulled into the driveway, surprised to see Marc's car there. Ravyn groaned. She was sure they were going to argue about the dog.

Marc opened the front door and came out onto the porch.

"Where were you?" he asked.

"At your brother's apartment, getting Blaze."

Ravyn got Harper out of her car seat and grabbed Blaze's leash to guide him into the house.

"What the hell is that mangy dog doing here? He is not coming into this house!"

"Well, yes he is."

"No, he's not!" Marc shouted.

"Keep your voice down. I need to get Harper back to bed."

"Why are you out so late?"

"Bruce called. He's been arrested for DUI, and he needed me to get his dog," Ravyn said, angry with her husband and his attitude. "Or did you want the dog to starve? Is that what you want?"

"Of course I don't want the dog to starve. But I don't want him in my house."

"YOUR house? I thought this was OUR house. Or am I just a guest? Is that what I am?"

Ravyn dragged the dog and her daughter into the house, shouldering her husband out of the doorway. She was furious now.

She put Harper back in her crib, towing the dog by his leash. Blaze cowered as he passed Marc.

"You are not a guest in this house. You are my wife," Marc shouted. "But I do not want that flea-bitten dog in here!"

"Well fuck you, Marc! The dog is here until Bruce can get him back. He can stay in the guest room, which is where I will be tonight!"

Ravyn stormed into the guest room, put Blaze in there, and closed the door. Then she went to her bedroom, got her pajamas, and went back to the guest room, slamming the door behind her.

Harper began to wail at the loud slam.

"Your daughter is crying!" Marc shouted.

"Deal with it!" Ravyn screamed through the door. "She's your daughter, too!"

Ravyn tossed and turned in the guest bed that night. She was so angry with Marc. How dare he tell her Blaze couldn't stay in the house. Where the hell was she supposed to bring the dog? It was cold outside. She certainly couldn't leave him tied up outside.

Blaze snuggled up next to her in the bed. He smelled. She'd have to give him a bath or take him to a groomer. He probably did have fleas. Bruce probably couldn't afford flea medicine if he didn't have any furniture and spent his money on alcohol and takeout food.

She probably would need to ask a vet about heartworm medicine, too. Her mind whirled about what it meant to be a dog owner. She'd only ever had cats.

Ravyn kept thinking she'd have to bring Blaze to her vet to get a full workover. She finally fell asleep with her arm wrapped around Blaze.

She awoke disoriented. She wasn't in her bed. She realized she was in the guest bed, then realized why she was there. Blaze was up and by the door, whining.

"Oh! You need to go out, don't you?"

Ravyn jumped up and grabbed his collar, holding onto him as she opened the guest bedroom door and got his make-do leash. She got him out the side door just in time and he did his business in the backyard. Ravyn realized she'd have to get some doggy waste bags.

Ravyn was mentally working on a list for Blaze: new leash, doggy waste bags, heartworm and flea medicine, dog shampoo. She'd neglected to grab his water and food bowls, so she added that to her mental list.

Ravyn got back in the house, stomping her feet to warm up. She sensed Marc wasn't in the house. She couldn't smell fresh coffee in the maker.

"Marc?" she called out. Silence responded.

Ravyn frowned again, angry. He expected her to take care of Harper and Blaze all by herself. He probably thought it was just punishment. She wasn't liking Marc very much these days.

She desperately wanted to call in a work-from-home day, but she knew she couldn't. She'd have to get Harper to daycare. Ravyn had no idea what to do with Blaze. She was afraid Marc would come back to the house and do heaven knows what with him.

Ravyn got the food out for Blaze just as Felix came out of Harper's room for his dinner. Felix arched his back at the sight of the dog. Blaze growled at Felix, thinking Felix was going to eat his food.

Blaze barked at Felix, who shot back into Harper's bedroom.

"Oh, for heaven's sake. I don't need this today," Ravyn said under her breath. She filled Felix's food bowl and brought it and his water bowl into Harper's room, putting it down and shutting the door.

One crisis averted. Now what to do with Blaze? She called a couple of doggy daycare places, but they needed proof of vaccines and Ravyn had no idea if Blaze had his shots or not.

Ravyn got Harper ready for daycare and then looked at Blaze. "OK, buddy, you are going to have to stay in the spare bathroom until I come home."

She put water in an old bowl and shut Blaze in the bathroom. He began to whine and whimper. She released Felix from Harper's room and hoped Felix wouldn't terrorize Blaze from under the bathroom door.

Ravyn prayed Blaze would be at the house when she returned that evening.

Ravyn was frazzled when she got home. She'd gone to the pet supermarket to get food bowls, a better leash, doggy waste bags, dog shampoo, and flea medicine before she picked up Harper.

When she got home, she was relieved she didn't see Marc's car in the driveway.

Ravyn got Harper situated in her playpen before checking on Blaze. She opened the guest bathroom door and gasped.

Blaze had shredded the shower curtain, eaten some of it, and thrown it up. He'd also peed on the floor and pooped.

"Oh, Blaze. Whew! That's a terrible smell. Let's get the floor cleaned up and then I'll give you a bath."

Then she noticed the bathroom door. Blaze had scratched at it, putting deep ruts on the inside of the door.

"Oh, God. Marc is going to kill you and then me."

She cleaned up the bathroom floor, thankful for the tile. Then she filled up the bathtub, putting dog shampoo in the water. Ravyn had never given a dog a bath before. She was hoping it wasn't as bad as trying to bathe Felix. She'd done that just once and barely escaped unscathed.

"OK, buddy, get in the tub," she said to Blaze. Blaze just looked at her. She picked him up and put all four paws in the water, but he jumped out, running out into the living room, and jumping into Harper's playpen, knocking her over.

Harper began to cry, but Blaze began to lick her face. Harper then began to squeal and laugh in her high-pitched laugh of delight.

Ravyn's heart began to beat normally again when she saw the pair in the playpen.

"OK. How about we try that again?" She put the leash on Blaze and held tight as she put him back in the bathroom. She then dragged the playpen to the door of the bathroom, blocking Blaze's exit. She could still see the ruts on the inside of the door. Could she just paint over it?

She was hoping Harper would be a good distraction for Blaze. She was right.

Ravyn got Blaze back in the bathtub and scrubbed him all over as Harper squealed with delight, clapping her hands.

"Doggy? This is a doggy, Harper," Ravyn said, pointing to Blaze. "His name is Blaze. Can you say doggy?"

Ravyn rinsed Blaze with warm water and began to reach for one of the guest bath towels hanging on the rod when he leaped out of the tub and shook himself off, getting both Ravyn and Harper wet. Harper blinked for a moment, then began laughing again.

"Well, at least you smell better, Blaze. In fact, we all smell better."

Ravyn got Harper, Blaze and Felix fed. She put flea medicine on Blaze's fur, and for good measure, gave a flea dose to Felix as well.

Felix scrambled under the guest bed as Blaze began to give chase. Blaze barked at Felix under the bed, who returned the barking with a hiss.

"OK, you two. Break it up."

Felix scurried into Harper's room and Ravyn shut the door. She was going to have to keep both animals apart for the time being.

Ravyn poured herself a generous glass of red wine that night, then another. She once again slept in the guest bedroom, since she wanted to keep Blaze out of the master bedroom until she was sure the flea medicine had taken effect. She had no trouble falling asleep with Blaze by her side.

Marc opened the guest bedroom door to a low growl from Blaze. The growl awoke Ravyn with a start, who sat straight up in the bed.

"Why is that mutt still here?" Marc demanded to know, pointing at Blaze, who continued to growl.

"Where else would he go?" Ravyn shot back, exasperated.

"I really don't want him here."

"Until Bruce is out of jail and back home, he's going to have to stay here."

"My mother paid Bruce's bond money. He's out of jail."

Ravyn pushed her messy hair from her face. "That's good news, right? Is he back at his apartment?"

"He's not going back to his apartment. My mother told him the only way she'd agree to his bond is if Bruce went straight into rehab again. She took him to an in-treatment facility in Midtown. He'll stay there for treatment."

"And when he comes out, he'll go back to his apartment? Because I went there. It's not a great place."

"You went there by yourself?"

"I had to, to get Blaze."

"Don't go there again alone. Bruce isn't going back there either," Marc said, his voice darker. "He's going to move in with my mother. She's going to let him live rent-free at the house."

"Maybe that's what he needs to get back on his feet."

"He needs a good swift kick in the ass."

"I'm guessing you aren't happy about him living in your old house."

"No, I'm not. And I'm not happy about this dog living here."

"Maybe Blaze can live with Bruce in Dunwoody when he's out of rehab."

"My mother is allergic to dogs. It's why we never had one growing up."

"Oh. Well, he won't live with your mother forever, right? He'll get his own place again."

"You don't know my brother very well. If he doesn't have to pay rent, he'll live with my mother as long as he can. She's always coddled him."

"I'm guessing that makes you unhappy."

"It makes me unhappy that he's a drunk and a deadbeat."

"Why should you care if he's living with your mother? Your home is supposed to be here."

"What's that supposed to mean?"

"Well, you haven't been here a lot lately. I've been getting Harper to daycare and picking her up. You haven't even come home to our bed!"

Ravyn had gotten out of bed and was shouting at Marc, who was shouting back. Blaze began barking and then Harper began wailing through the baby monitor.

"Aren't you going to get Harper?" Marc shouted.

"That's just great! You once said you would never be like your father. Well, guess what?! You are acting a lot like him right now!"

Marc's mouth dropped open, looking as if he'd been slapped. He turned and walked toward the front door.

Ravyn was shocked at what she had said and walked behind Marc, grabbing his arm at the door. "I'm sorry. I didn't mean that. I was angry with you."

"You meant every word of it, Ravyn. Every word."

"Where are you going?"

"Back to my mother's house. At least I know I'm loved and welcomed there!"

"You are loved and welcomed here!" she shouted. "Marc! Don't leave!"

Marc slammed the front door, rattling the frame and making a wall mirror fall off, smashing into pieces on the floor. Ravyn sat behind the closed front door and cried.

Chapter 10

Ravyn called Julie in tears. She recounted her fight with Marc in gulping breaths. She'd gotten Harper calmed down, but Blaze barked intermittently in the background.

"What is going on at your house?"

"It's pretty much chaos now."

"Welcome to motherhood, Ravyn. Taking care of the children always falls to the mother, no matter how much the fathers say they are going to be involved."

"I said something terrible to Marc, though."

Ravyn told Julie how she'd compared Marc to his own deceased uninvolved father. She recounted how Marc had stormed out of the house and then she began crying again. Hearing her mother crying, Harper began crying again.

"I know you can tell me to mind my own business, Ravyn, but do you think you and Marc should go to a marriage counselor? You both probably could use better communication skills. And he may need some grief counseling."

"I don't think Marc would agree to go. He's so angry."

"He probably needs it most of all. Anger management and all that. If he won't go, you should."

"Alone?"

"I've been going to therapy since the divorce and it's wonderful to talk out my problems, worries, and issues. My counselor gives me constructive things to think about. I'm still mad as hell at my asshole ex-husband, but I no longer want to kill him."

"That's good to know. I'm not sure we could make it look like an accident."

"There's the Ravyn I know and love. Helping me bury the body."

"Is your therapist taking new clients?"

"I really don't know, but I'll text you her number."

Ravyn hung up with Julie, feeling better. She got Harper fed and dressed in warm clothes, put her in the jogging stroller, and grabbed Blaze's new leash. She was going to run her frustration out this morning, even if it would make her late for work.

She got everyone out the door and began running hard. Blaze ran along but had never really run with a jogger and wanted to constantly run in front of the stroller. Ravyn shortened his lead and kept him closer to her on the left. Blaze eventually got into her rhythm. By the time they got back to the house, Blaze was panting, and Harper was asleep.

Ravyn got water for Blaze, put Harper in the crib, and quickly took a shower. Now dressed and ready for work, Ravyn loaded Harper in her car seat and headed to daycare before continuing to work an hour and a half late.

Ravyn was unsure about calling a counselor. She tried to ask other co-workers if they had ever sought counseling. She started with the magazine's art director Chase Riley.

"Chase, have you or your wife ever sought a counselor? I mean through work?"

Chase looked surprised, but then said, "Well, I'm not sure you know this, but my wife had a miscarriage about a year and a half ago. She went to counseling. I mean, I went as well, but she went a little longer than I did."

"Oh, Chase. I'm so sorry. I didn't know that. I'm really sorry for your loss."

"We got through it, and Mandi needed it a bit more than I did. Don't get me wrong, it was bad for both of us, but as a woman, I'm guessing it was worse for her. Maybe I'm not saying it right."

"No, I think I understand what you're saying. And Mandi is on your healthcare plan?"

"She is."

"Was the process pretty easy?"

"Actually, it was calling around a lot of places to see if they were accepting new clients and to see if they took our insurance. Are you OK?"

"I'm not sure. Marc's father died recently and he's taking it badly and I just think we both probably need to talk to someone. I'm not sure if he would go. I haven't asked him yet. Please don't say anything to anyone."

"Of course I won't. And I haven't told many people in the office about our miscarriage."

"Chase, I won't say anything to anyone. I'm glad you shared your experience with me and I'm really sorry that happened to you and Mandi."

"Well — and we haven't told anyone this yet either, so please don't say anything — but we're pregnant again."

Ravyn could feel her eyes well up with tears. "That's wonderful!"

"It's early days. We're not going to make any kind of announcement until she's further along. We just want to wait to tell everyone in the office."

"I completely understand. I won't say anything, but I'm really happy for you both."

"I hope you and Marc can talk to someone, too, if that's what you want to do. Just start calling places now. They often don't have available appointments right away, either."

"That's great advice. Thanks for your help and your honesty."

Ravyn returned to her office and began searching the internet and writing down numbers of some counseling services in Midtown, Buckhead, and Dunwoody.

She hoped whenever Marc showed up back at the house, she could discuss it with him without him blowing up about it.

Ravyn picked Harper up from daycare and headed home. She was disappointed she did not see Marc's BMW in the driveway.

She walked into the house and could tell Marc had been there. She found one of his shirt drawers partially opened and some of his shirts gone. Ravyn, however, did not find any note from him. Nothing to indicate how long he would be gone. She found his behavior so maddening.

Ravyn changed into her running clothes, put Harper in the jogging stroller again, and grabbed the leash for Blaze. She intended to run out her frustration again this evening.

Ravyn noticed a large scratch on Blaze's nose. She guessed he had tangled with Felix and lost. "Sorry Blaze. Guess Felix let you know who's boss."

Ravyn got her lighted safety vest on and headed out the door. She realized on her run she'd have to buy a lighted harness for Blaze as well. Maybe something for Harper, too. It was one thing to run in the neighborhood by herself, but quite another to have a dark stroller and a dog with her.

When Ravyn got home, she fed Blaze and Harper, then fixed a light supper for herself. She again poured herself a glass of red wine. Taking Harper and Blaze for a run every morning and evening, Ravyn would certainly work off the last of her baby weight.

Take that, Laura! Ravyn thought as she sipped her wine.

Ravyn was watching TV, Blaze snuggled next to her on the couch when she heard the lock on the front door. She turned to see Marc.

"You're home," she said.

"Yeah. My mother kicked me out."

"Kicked you out?"

"She said I shouldn't be spending so much time with her. That I should be home with you and Harper."

"Wise woman."

Marc said nothing, scowled and walked into the master bedroom. He came out with his gym bag. "I'm going to the gym."

"Can we please talk before you bolt out of here again?"

"Bolt out of here?"

"I'd like for us to see a marriage counselor."

"A what? A marriage counselor? Why the hell should we see one? Nothing is wrong with our marriage."

"Marc, you've been avoiding me, this house, and our daughter. I think we need some counseling. I think you need to talk about what's bothering you."

"Just me? What about you? Bringing this dog into our house without even talking to me about it."

Blaze began his low growl at Marc.

"That fucking dog doesn't even like me!"

"Marc, I think he senses you don't like him either."

"I'm not going to a counselor and that's final." Marc slammed the front door on his way out.

Ravyn began to cry. Blaze laid his head into her lap. She stroked his head and drank more of her wine.

Ravyn slept in the guest bedroom that night, snuggled next to Blaze. Since his bath, he didn't smell nearly as bad. And now that he was eating better food, he also wasn't farting as much.

She got up the next morning, got Harper up, fed her, and got Harper and Blaze both ready for a run. She peeked into the master bedroom but noticed the bed hadn't been slept in.

Ravyn sighed. She hoped Blaze and Harper were ready for a long, hard run.

When she got to her office she called Julie, who answered crying.

"What's wrong? Are you OK? Are the girls OK?"

"The girls are fine. It's me. I'm not OK."

"What's wrong?"

"You know my asshole ex moved his girlfriend into my house, right?"

"Yes."

"The girls told me the asshole and the homewrecker are getting married next month. They are to be the flower girls. They are excited about it. I'm devastated."

"Julie, I'm so sorry. I don't know what to say."

"I know I just need to move on, but I really don't know how to do that. I'm glad I'm meeting my therapist later this afternoon."

"Speaking of therapists, I tried to talk to Marc about seeing a counselor and he got defensive and mad and went to the gym and didn't come home last night. I'm going to have to go by myself."

"I'm sorry for you, too. Did you call my therapist?"

"No, but I'm going to."

"Sounds like we need a girl's night out."

"We most certainly do, or at least I do, but you are forgetting my husband is MIA."

"Hmm. Well, I'll need a babysitter as well. What if I hire the babysitter for my girls and you can bring Harper over? He can watch all three."

"He?"

"Oh, my girls have a little crush on him, but he's really good. He knows infant and child CPR. We can go to Seven Lamps. That's not far from my apartment, so we'll be close. We can Uber there. You can stay over if you need to."

"Well, with the dog, I can't stay over. Why don't I Uber to your apartment and then we Uber to the restaurant and I can Uber back home? That way I can drink, and no one drives."

"Sounds like a plan. Want to do it Friday or Saturday?"

"Either night. I'm sure Marc will still be wherever he goes to avoid me."

"Call my therapist right after you hang up with me."

"I will."

"Hang in there, Ravyn. I believe in you and Marc. You are just going through a rough patch."

"I hope you are right. I just didn't think it would be this hard so soon. Harper's not even a year old yet."

"Oh my God! Her birthday's coming up! What? In three weeks?"

"Actually, two weeks. Let's just hope her mother and father are on speaking terms by then."

Ravyn called Julie's therapist and was glad to get an initial appointment at the end of February. She drove back to daycare feeling lighter and happier. She was glad she was going to be able to talk to someone about her feelings.

She picked up Harper and drove home, once again feeding Harper, then getting her into the jogging stroller and hooking Blaze to his leash.

Ravyn was running hard, Blaze on her left, keeping up with her. She thought he enjoyed the run as much as she did. Harper just loved the run, kicking her feet and shrieking her delight as they ran the neighborhood.

Ravyn had gotten Blaze a lighted leash and had gotten flashing lights for the stroller. They were well lit on the run. Ravyn felt safer on the road.

She got home, fed and watered Blaze, and got Harper down for the night. Ravyn started a fire, then she poured herself a large glass of red wine while Blaze snuggled up next to her on the couch. Felix came creeping around the corner and hissed at Blaze but even Felix settled on the far end of the couch.

Everyone was sleepy in front of the fire, its warm glow relaxing them. The fire was soothing.

Ravyn awoke with a start to a smoky living room and Blaze barking wildly. The smoke detectors were now blaring, and she could hear Harper begin to cry through the monitor.

Ravyn jumped up from the couch, knocking her wine glass over, shattering it on the hardwood floor. She grabbed Harper from her crib and opened the front door, trying to let some of the smoke out.

Blaze continued to bark and Ravyn searched frantically for her phone, holding Harper on her hip. Ravyn found her phone near the couch but managed to step in the broken wine glass, cutting her foot.

She hopped out onto the front porch, dialing 911 to report the fire. Although she never did see fire. She only saw smoke.

In what seemed like time standing still, Ravyn could finally hear emergency sirens and the all too familiar fire trucks pulling up in front of her house.

Blaze growled as the firefighters came onto the front porch.

"Blaze!" Ravyn shouted. She grabbed him by the collar and pulled him around to the side of the yard. Harper wailed at the chaotic scene, red lights flashing, firefighters pulling hoses from the truck.

A police officer walked over to Ravyn, asking what had happened. Ravyn related her dog woke her up and there was smoke in the living room. Then the smoke detectors sounded.

A firefighter also came up to them.

"We don't find any evidence of a fire right now," she said. "But we think you may have had a bird's nest in your chimney. That probably caught fire, so you will want to have your chimney inspected. Could have been soot buildup, too. We're going to hose down the roof just to be sure there aren't any embers from the chimney."

"But we've used the fireplace before tonight. Would a bird have built a nest that quickly?"

"Could be a squirrel's nest," the firefighter responded. "They can build them pretty fast. But when was the last time you had your chimney inspected? I'd recommend you do that before you use the fireplace again."

Ravyn shifted Harper on her hip and winced when she put her right foot down.

"What's the matter?"

"I broke a wine glass on the floor in the commotion and I stepped on it. I think I may have glass in my foot."

"Here, let me see," the firefighter said.

The police officer took Harper from Ravyn and Ravyn sat on the curb, the firefighter shining her flashlight on the bottom of Ravyn's foot.

"Ma'am, it looks like you do have glass in that foot. You'll need to go to the hospital to see if they can take it out."

"Can't you just pull it out with some tweezers or something?"

"Can't do that, ma'am. Don't know how deep it is or if there is any ligament damage."

Ravyn could feel herself beginning to panic. How was she going to get herself and Harper to the emergency room? It was her right foot that was injured. Could she still drive?

"I'll have to drive myself there," Ravyn said, her voice cracking.

"I'd advise against that. Can a friend drive you? Your husband?"

"My husband is away at the moment. It's so late, I don't want to disturb my neighbors. And I'd have to put Harper in her car seat."

"We can call an ambulance."

"But my daughter. I can't leave her here. And I'll have to put the dog back in the house. I'll need to do that once everyone leaves."

"Again, I'd advise you not to drive yourself, but I can't stop you," the firefighter said.

"OK. Once everyone leaves, I'll get the dog settled."

About an hour and a half later, the fire trucks pulled away from her house. Ravyn hobbled up the steps to the front porch, her foot stinging with pain.

She put Harper back in her crib and put Blaze in the guest bedroom. She called out to Felix, even rattling his treat box to see if he'd come out from wherever he was hiding.

No Felix. Ravyn was worried that in the hubbub of the firefighters in and out of her house, that Felix had slipped out. He was a strictly indoor cat, and she was worried she couldn't find him.

"Felix! Felix!" she called.

Ravyn went into the master bathroom and got her own set of tweezers out and looked at the bottom of her foot. The glass was embedded in her foot, but it was thin. Maybe she could just yank it out.

Ravyn sucked in a deep breath and held it, pulling on the glass. She yelped as it came out, but her foot began to bleed badly.

It reminded her of her accident in Mexico when she also stepped on broken glass at the beach. It had also been her right foot. She was probably going to need stitches. The cut looked deep.

Ravyn wrapped her foot in a towel, trying to stem the bleeding. She limped into the kitchen and got a plastic bag and stuck her foot in it. She didn't want to bleed all over the house.

She wrapped some tape around the bag, enclosing her foot, then limped back to Harper's room. Harper was sound asleep in her crib.

"I'm sorry baby girl. Mommy's got to see about this hurt foot," she said, lifting her daughter out of the crib and grabbing her blanket.

Of all nights when Marc wasn't here! Ravyn cursed him under her breath. Where the hell was he? Ravyn got Harper in her car seat, got in the driver's seat, and pulled out of the driveway into the dark night, headed for Piedmont Hospital.

Ravyn was nearly asleep when the nurse finally called her back into a treatment room. Harper was a solid sleeping lump in Ravyn's lap. The nurse took Harper and laid her down on the exam table. Harper barely moved.

Ravyn could see the clock on the wall said 3:16 a.m. Had she really been waiting for three hours?

A physician's assistant cleaned the wound, putting just a few quick stitches in the foot before closing it for good with steri strips. He then bandaged her foot. A doctor then came to check on her and wrote a prescription for some antibiotics, and a topical cream.

She was told to keep the foot dry for the next two days and to try to stay off it as much as she could. He then released her.

Ravyn gathered Harper and headed to pay her bill. She reached into her handbag for her wallet and saw her phone had several missed messages, all from Marc.

She was so pissed at him, she didn't even listen to the voicemails. She just got in her car and drove home.

"Where have you been?" Marc demanded when Ravyn pulled up in the driveway. "I've been trying to call you. Don't you answer your phone? What happened to the house? Why does it smell like smoke?"

"I was at the hospital, Marc. I cut my foot on some glass in the living room after there was a fire."

"A fire? What fire?!"

"The firefighters think a squirrel's nest or a bird's nest caught fire in the chimney. They came and checked everything out and I had to take me and Harper to the emergency room to get stitches in my foot because *YOU* weren't here to help. I might ask you where *you've* been?"

"I got home to find an empty house, blood on the floor. God, I was worried. Why didn't you answer your phone?"

"I was in the emergency room, Marc, with Harper!"

"I'm sorry. I should have been here. Why was Felix outside?"

"You found him? Oh, thank God!" Ravyn started to cry with relief and exhaustion.

"I see that dog is still here," Marc griped.

Ravyn turned, suddenly angry. "You should be damn glad he is still here. He's the one who began barking when the living room filled up with smoke! He woke me up!"

"Why didn't the smoke detectors go off?"

"They did, but not before Blaze began barking. I'm exhausted. I'm putting Harper back to bed and then I'm going to bed."

"What about me?"

"You can go to hell for all I care."

Chapter 11

Ravyn slept in the master bedroom with Blaze, while Marc slept in the guest bedroom. Ravyn awoke to a dog licking her face and a throbbing right foot.

Marc awoke to a morning erection and a desire to have sex with his wife. It had been a long time, he thought. Probably his fault, but still.

Ravyn hobbled out of the bedroom. She realized her run with Harper and Blaze would be delayed by a few days, if not weeks, but Blaze still needed a walk. She put food in his bowl and started the coffee maker. She was going to need it this morning. Ravyn wasn't quite sure how well she was going to function at work today.

At least Marc might take Harper to daycare this morning. She hoped.

Marc wandered out of the guest room and said nothing as he poured a cup of coffee. He wasn't sure if he wanted to talk to Ravyn after she told him to go to hell the night before.

"Are you taking Harper to daycare today or am I doing it?" Ravyn asked, getting Harper fed in her high chair.

"I can take her."

"Thank you. Then I can take Blaze for a walk."

"Why are you taking that mutt for a walk?"

"Because he needs exercise, Marc. When you weren't here, I was taking Harper and Blaze for a run every morning and every evening."

Marc was silent again. He took a sip of coffee. "That's a lot of exercise."

"It is, but I was enjoying it until I stepped on the glass."

"I'm sorry you hurt your foot, Ravyn. I'm sorry I wasn't here. It's just…"

"Just what?" Ravyn asked, irritated.

"It's just I'm feeling our relationship has changed."

"Of course it has changed!" Ravyn shouted. "I've been trying to be understanding, but you stay at your mother's house rather than be with me or your daughter. I feel like a single mother!"

"You are not a single mother! I am very much a part of this family!"

"Are you, Marc? You act as if you can't be bothered. Like you'd rather be single again!"

"I don't want to be single! I want to be married! To you, dammit! I want to come home and have dinner with my wife and make love to her at night."

"Is that all you see me as?" Ravyn shouted. "Someone who will cook for you, and you can have sex with?"

"That's not what I said! I just want to go back to a loving relationship!"

"And yet you won't go to marriage counseling! Well, I've made an appointment and I'm going *BY MYSELF*! Because you don't want to! I wanted you to come with me so we can get back to where we were."

"Are you really going alone?"

"Of course! I'm doing *EVERYTHING* alone these days!"

With all the shouting, Harper began to cry, and Blaze began to bark and growl.

Ravyn grabbed the leash for Blaze and her coat, which she put over her pajamas. "Come on, Blaze. Let's go for a walk. *ALONE*."

When Ravyn returned home, after a brisk walk around the neighborhood, looking somewhat crazy in just pajamas, slippers, and her coat. Rather, it was as brisk as Ravyn's foot could take, but it was cold outside.

Blaze tried to run, but Ravyn held him back on his leash. If she wasn't so angry with Marc she would have put on her sweatpants and sweatshirt, at least.

She came home to an empty house. Marc and Harper were nowhere to be found. She didn't even get to say goodbye to her daughter. Ravyn put the leash up and began to cry. This was not how she wanted to live her married life.

Ravyn took a shower with her foot sealed in a plastic bag, got dressed, and headed off to work, on time, she realized.

Ravyn worked with her foot, in just a sock, propped up on her extra office chair and when it came time to go home, she texted Marc that she was going to pick up Harper. Would Marc be home for dinner or would be he spending the evening at his mother's house?

She knew she was being passive-aggressive, but it felt good.

Ravyn didn't get an answer from Marc, so she headed to Colony Square to pick up Harper. She then got home and got Harper into the jogging stroller and the leash on Blaze.

Again, Blaze wanted to run, but Ravyn pulled him back to just a brisk walk. Her foot hurt with every step, but she'd worn a running shoe on her left foot and a slipper on her right foot. It looked silly, but it worked.

Ravyn started to think about her future counseling appointment at the end of the month. She still would rather Marc go with her. But she was looking forward to talking — or rather complaining — to the counselor about Marc.

She hoped the counselor would take her side. Why not? Marc wasn't going to be there to defend himself. She could make him look as horrible as she felt he was being.

But what if the counselor talked about compromising with him? Ravyn felt like she was doing all the compromising.

Ravyn got back to the house feeling like a dark cloud was over her head.

When she heard the front door open, she was halfway through getting dinner ready. Harper was starting to eat more solid food, but it had to be cut up into small pieces. Marc came into the kitchen and said how good dinner smelled.

Ravyn half-smiled. She knew she cooked a good meal. She had a chicken breast sautéing on the stove, with potatoes ready to go in the microwave, and was ready to start sautéing Brussel sprouts.

Harper would get green peas instead of Brussel sprouts. Ravyn had seen the face Harper had made when she tasted them for the first time.

Ravyn reached into the refrigerator for another chicken breast and put it in the sauté pan.

She just wanted a nice meal with Marc and Harper without any shouting or drama. Was that too much to ask? Ravyn felt like she was walking on eggshells, watching what she said during dinner, only making small talk, trying to smile when she felt like bursting into tears.

Marc helped Ravyn clean up. He even washed the pans while Ravyn got Harper ready for bed.

When Ravyn got Harper settled, she came out to the living room to Marc holding two glasses of wine.

"I'd start a fire, but I guess that's not a good idea."

"The fire department said we should have the chimney inspected before we use it again. Something about soot build-up. Have you ever had the chimney inspected?"

"It's a gas fireplace. I didn't think I needed to."

"Well, the firefighter said we ought to."

"OK, so no romantic fire tonight."

Blaze padded into the living room and sniffed his dog bed. Felix was curled up in it. Felix yawned, then hissed at Blaze. Blaze walked twice around his bed, then put his two front paws in the bed.

Felix hissed again and Blaze got out of the bed, circling the bed again, then put his hindquarters in the bed and was half in and half out of the bed.

"Poor Blaze. Is Felix in your bed? Felix, get out of Blaze's bed."

Felix didn't move and neither did Blaze. Ravyn was pleasantly surprised they were starting to get along.

"I'm not sure how romantic the evening will be with the dog and cat in here," Marc said.

"Are we being romantic tonight?"

"I'm trying to be," he said, handing over Ravyn's wine as she settled on the couch and propped her foot up on the coffee table.

Marc sat on the couch next to Ravyn and put his arm around her shoulder. Ravyn curled into him. He smelled good. He was wearing the cologne she loved.

"I've missed this," she whispered, putting her head on his shoulder.

"Me too."

Marc stroked Ravyn's hair, eventually ducking his head to kiss her lightly on the lips. Then he kissed her more deeply.

Ravyn responded to his kisses, embracing him, and moving on top of him on the couch. It had been so long since they'd made love. She felt her body respond to his kisses, to his touch.

Marc ran his hands through her hair, and she felt sparks not only from the static electricity but also the sparks now coursing through her body.

"Let's go to the bedroom," he murmured.

"I'm ready to take you right here on this couch," she replied.

"Bedroom. I don't want that dog barking or growling at what I'm about to do to you."

Ravyn hadn't slept that well in a long time. She smiled as she thought about how she and Marc had made love the night before.

She now understood the term mad passionate love. That's what it was. Beneath the surface, they were still angry with one another, and their lovemaking was rough at first, but then they became tender with one another.

Marc had thrust hard into her, making Ravyn cry out in pain.

"I'm sorry. I'm so sorry," he whispered as he held her tight. Then he began to be gentler with her, his long strokes penetrating deeply.

Ravyn bent her knees as he stroked into her, and she felt a wave of her orgasm. Now she cried out with pleasure.

Ravyn was sore the next morning. She rolled over and nuzzled Marc's back.

"Good morning, lover."

Marc rolled over to face her. "Good morning to you, too."

"Can we play hooky today? Stay in bed and make love all day?"

"I'd love to, but you have to go to work, and so do I. Can we take a raincheck until Saturday morning? Then you and I can lay in bed until Harper wakes us up. Which I'm sure will still be long before we want to get up."

"Party pooper." Ravyn rolled out of bed and grabbed her robe. "I'll get the coffee started."

Marc rolled over and grabbed his phone. "Oh shit."

"What?"

"I turned my phone off last night. There are lots of missed calls from my mother, and then her neighbor."

Marc tried calling his mother, but the call went to voicemail. Then he tried the neighbor.

"Oh my God! Is she alright? OK, I'm on my way to the hospital now."

"What happened? What's wrong?"

"My mother fell in the house. She broke her hip. She lay on the floor until she could crawl to her phone. She's at Northside. I've got to go."

"Oh my God! Of course. Let me know how she is. Give her our love."

Marc quickly got dressed and left the house. Ravyn sighed. She would have to get Blaze out for his walk and Harper to school. And she would have to do it by herself.

Ravyn put on her sweats, got Harper fed, then bundled her up for a morning walk in the jogging stroller. She grabbed the leash for Blaze, but he knew the routine. He was already at the door ready to go.

Back at the house, she fed Blaze and quickly took her shower. She got Harper loaded in the car and was on the road in time for heavy morning traffic. Ravyn was late to work and pulled out her makeup bag to put on the rest of her makeup.

Ravyn felt like she was falling down at her job. She was behind on a couple of deadlines, and she was trying to be a good mother, too. Being a working mother was way harder than she ever expected.

She called Marc mid-morning to get an update on his mother and to ask if he'd be home for dinner.

Marc said his mother fell in the dining room on the hardwood floors and broke her right hip and wrist. She'd tried to catch herself as she fell. Carol was going to be in the hospital for at least a week, then she'd be released to a rehabilitation facility for at least a week, then home.

Marc expected he'd be home for dinner but would return to the hospital until visiting hours were over. He'd be back and forth to the hospital while she was there, then he would visit her at the rehabilitation facility.

Once his mother got home, they'd have some decisions to make. He didn't elaborate on what those decisions would be.

Ravyn got emails out to her freelancers with story ideas for the April issue. There were new restaurants expected to open and this issue would focus on spring fashion.

She emailed Julie, too, to see if she wanted an assignment, but didn't hear back right away. Ravyn would call her later that night. They hadn't spoken in a while.

Ravyn looked up and realized she'd be late to pick up Harper if she didn't leave right away. She sprinted as best she could with her foot and got to Harper's daycare right before she'd be charged extra for being late.

At home, she changed clothes, put Harper in the jogging stroller, and grabbed Blaze's leash. She walked as quickly as she could. Her foot was healing, she could tell. She was glad she was nearly done with her antibiotics. They were making her stomach upset.

Ravyn got dinner started and Marc arrived about seven o'clock. He looked exhausted.

"You look like you could use a scotch."

"I'd love one. What did you fix for dinner?"

"I've got salmon I'm putting in the oven in about 10 minutes. Fix your scotch."

Marc walked to the small bar and pulled down a low-ball glass, got ice from the refrigerator, then poured himself a few fingers of scotch.

Marc drank a couple of scotches and after dinner, he headed to bed. By the time Ravyn got Harper fed and in bed, she found Marc sound asleep in the bed, snoring.

So much for making mad passionate love that evening. She was disappointed. She had hoped they were back on track, but now she wasn't so sure.

The next morning, Marc took Harper to daycare before he headed to the hospital. Ravyn was grateful she could just get Blaze out for his walk and not have to worry about being late for work.

When she got to her office, Ravyn called Julie. She'd forgotten to call her the night before and she needed to know if she wanted the freelance assignment.

"Julie, have I caught you at a bad time? I haven't heard from you, and I need to know if you'd like that freelance assignment."

"Oh Ravyn," Julie said tearfully.

"What's the matter? What's happened?"

"The homewrecker is pregnant! And she's going to have a boy. That's why Rob and that bitch are getting married so soon. She gave him the son I couldn't."

Julie sobbed into the phone as Ravyn tried to console her.

"Did he tell you she's pregnant?"

"He told the girls last weekend when he had them. They told me. And the worst part for me is they are excited to have a baby brother. Oh, Ravyn," her voice trailed off to more crying.

"I'm so sorry, Julie. I'm just so sorry. This just isn't fair."

"Who said life was fair?"

"We should have that dinner we meant to have. I'll buy the first round."

"We better take Uber because I'll be getting drunk. If we do it in a couple of weeks, Rob will have the girls again."

"Sounds like a plan. And I hate to ask this, but can you do the freelance assignment?"

"I'll take it. With the winter months, home showings have been slow, so they don't need me as much to stage houses. I'm still working on my real estate license. I really think I might be good at this."

"I think you'd be great at it. You have the personality for real estate."

"You're just saying that."

"No. When I was looking for a condo, my real estate agent had a great personality. And she didn't hold back. She told me what I could and could not afford. I think you can do that too. Find people what they want but tell them what they can't afford. I swear to God that was the best advice."

"I can't wait for our dinner. Should we go to Seven Lamps like we planned?"

"I'll make reservations. Oh, Marc's mother fell and broke her hip and wrist."

"What? When did that happen? Is he at your house or still at her house?"

"He came home the night before last. We had a big fight and then had really great sex. I mean really great sex."

"There is a fine line between love and hate."

"I don't hate him, Julie. I love him."

"No, I mean that being angry with each other can really stir up the passion. Sounds like that's what happened to you two."

"It did. Honestly, it was incredible. I just wish my foot didn't hurt so much."

"Your foot?"

"Oh God, we haven't talked for a while. There was a fire in the chimney. Blaze woke me up, but I knocked over my wine glass, and then stepped on the broken glass. Cut my foot."

"A fire? Is the house OK?"

"Fine. It just made a lot of smoke, but Blaze woke me up so I could get Harper out of the house."

"You still have Blaze? I thought Bruce would have him back by now."

"Bruce got arrested for DUI and is now in rehab. We have the dog. Temporarily. I think."

"Dinner can't come soon enough, Ravyn. What happened with your foot?"

"I ended up with a toddler at the emergency room at Piedmont after midnight, getting stitches."

"And the fire?"

"The firefighters think it was a squirrel's nest. No damage, thank God. Except for all that smoke. Blaze really kind of saved the day."

"And you are OK?"

"My foot is almost right as rain, and I'm just about done with the antibiotics."

"Ravyn, that incredible sex you and Marc had. He did wear a condom, didn't he?"

Ravyn was silent. "No. But I've only just stopped breastfeeding. You can't get pregnant when you're breastfeeding. I'm good, right?"

Now Julie was silent. "I hope you are good. Umm. You might want to take another pregnancy test."

"Oh, no no no no no. I am not pregnant again."

"OK. For your sake, I hope not. I know you wanted to space your children."

"I am going to space my children. I am not pregnant! Don't even think that! Don't even say that! I'm going to call about going back on the pill right away. You've got me worried."

"I'm sure you're fine. Just, before you go back on the pill, take a pregnancy test. Just to ease your mind."

"I'm about to cry, Julie. I do not want to be pregnant again. Not with the hard time I had with the first one. The bed rest and time off from work. I'm barely keeping it together being a working mother to one child. I'd lose my mind if I had to do it with two in diapers!"

"Calm down. It's probably nothing. Nothing! Just you and Marc be more careful until you go back on the pill."

Ravyn hung up with Julie, reserving a date and time for dinner at Seven Lamps, but couldn't shake the dread she might be pregnant again. On her lunch hour, she rushed to the pharmacy to buy a pregnancy test and took it in the ladies' room in her office. She nearly wept with joy when she saw it was negative.

Marc picked up Harper early that afternoon and had dinner on the stove by the time Ravyn got home.

"This is a nice surprise," she said, taking off her jacket. "Do I have time to take Blaze for a quick walk?"

"Sure."

"Harper, do you want to go for a walk with me and Blaze?"

"Baas," she said, pointing to Blaze.

"Is she saying that dog's name?" Marc asked.

"I think she is! She's learning so much now."

Marc and Ravyn watched in astonishment as Harper pushed herself up and took a few steps toward her stroller.

"My God! Her first steps!"

Harper fell on her butt after those first few steps. Ravyn picked up her daughter and gave her some kisses and a hug. "I'm glad we could see this together."

"Me, too. I had no idea she was walking."

"Well, toddling. I bet she'll be walking soon. We will have to baby-proof the house now. Most babies start to walk a little after their first year. Don't forget her birthday is next Sunday."

"I didn't forget. Are we having a party for her?"

"It's her first birthday. I think we should have a small party with just family. I'll ask my parents and sister and her family to come. We'll celebrate on Sunday. Do you think your mother will be able to come? Will she be out of the hospital by then?"

"She won't be."

"Will Bruce be out of rehab by then? We should ask him to come too. He loves Harper."

Marc grimaced. "He won't be out of rehab. It's a 28-day in-house program and he's only been there a little over a week."

"Please ask him. See if he can come for a couple of hours."

"He's only allowed to go to work. Can you believe he didn't get fired? He should have been. But since he went into rehab and has work release, he's still at Northside. I wonder about him being around all those drugs there."

"But he's the janitor. They keep those drugs locked up, right? He can't get at them."

"You don't know him. To get drugs he'll do just about anything. What if he sneaks into a patient's room and gets drugs that way?"

"Marc, when I gave birth, I had to beg for some painkillers, remember? They don't just leave them lying around. That nurse put that pill in my hand and watched me take it. Besides, he's getting treatment."

Marc shook his head. "He went to treatment before and it didn't help."

Ravyn clipped on Blaze's leash and put Harper in the jogging stroller. "We won't be too long. Maybe 20 minutes." She kissed Marc as she left the house.

Marc had the table set when she returned from her brisk walk. Her foot still ached, but the pain was less. Ravyn felt sure she'd be running again soon.

Baby Steps

When they'd finished dinner, Marc asked if he could go back to Northside Hospital to visit his mother before visiting hours were over.

Ravyn kissed him at the front door and said she'd clean up. "Give your mother our love. Tell her I'll come to visit soon. I'm sure I can't bring Harper to visit at the hospital. When will she be moved to the rehabilitation facility? Is it close to our house?"

"We're trying to figure that out. She needs to have better pain management, but they really do want to move her so she can get physical therapy. I just hate that she was alone when she fell. I should have been there."

Harper's birthday fell on a Sunday. Ravyn had picked up a fancy cupcake for Harper at a cupcake store at Lenox Square, a mall in Buckhead.

The day before, however, she bought a small cake at Publix for her and Marc to share at a little private party she'd planned. She also brought home a sheet cake and three containers of ice cream for the family she expected to arrive Sunday.

Ravyn had invited Julie and her girls to come as well. She'd asked for no gifts, but she already suspected her family and Julie wouldn't honor that request.

Ravyn got Blaze and Harper out for their morning brisk walk. It was nearly 40 degrees around 9 a.m. and the high was projected to be near 70 degrees later that afternoon. She was disappointed the weather wouldn't be as pleasant the next day. The late morning called for rain. She hoped her family wasn't going to drive in the rain.

Marc got home from the gym in the early afternoon and Ravyn had mylar Happy Birthday balloons tied to chairs in the dining room. She had Harper in a cute pink dress with white tights and even had a cardboard happy birthday tiara for her.

Harper didn't like the tiara that much, and Ravyn had to keep putting it on her head to try to get a cute picture. Ravyn thought it would be a cute Christmas newsletter photo.

Ravyn suddenly realized why she always rolled her eyes at her friends' Christmas newsletters. She'd likely have a photo with her, Harper, Marc, and Blaze on their Christmas card. And her friends would roll their eyes at her newsletter and Christmas card.

Ravyn inwardly giggled that Blaze was going to make it onto the Christmas card. Marc would roll his eyes at that.

Ravyn got Harper in her high chair and put the cupcake in front of her. She and Marc sang an off-key happy birthday to her, and Harper reached out to grab the frosting off the cupcake.

Ravyn cringed when Harper tried to put the frosting in her mouth, then wiped it down her pink dress.

Harper suddenly took her fist and grabbed a chunk of the cupcake and stuffed that in her mouth, smearing most of the frosting on her face. Then she wiped the rest of the cupcake in her hair.

Ravyn reached out to stop Harper, but Marc held her arm and smiled. He was recording it on his phone.

Next, Harper took her fist and smashed the rest of the cupcake before smearing it on the high chair tray before stuffing more of the cupcake in her mouth. Harper then gave her parents a toothy grin.

Blaze was loving the party, too. He was greedily gobbling up everything that fell to the floor. Harper realized she could just drop it down to Blaze.

Blaze then stood up on his hind legs, put his paws on Harper's high chair tray and snatched the remainder of the cupcake in his mouth. That elicited a cry of disappointment from Harper.

"Bad dog!" Marc said, trying to grab Blaze by his collar. Blaze growled at Marc.

"No, no, Baas, no!" Harper said, sternly, pointing at the dog.

Marc and Ravyn looked at each other. "I guess that's her first sentence!"

Ravyn got Blaze by his collar and put him in the guest bathroom, returning with a washcloth to wipe down Harper's face, hands, and hair. "I'd try to wipe down her dress, but really that needs to go in the washing machine. She really needs to have a bath, too. I feel like all I did was smear more of the frosting in her hair."

"It will be a cute video to play for your family tomorrow," Marc said.

"It will be a cute video to play at her wedding."

"I'm not ready to even think about that. She's not dating until she's 30."

Ravyn laughed. "Going to polish all of your shotguns when the boys come to take her to prom?"

"That's not a bad idea!"

"Well, now that we've ruined Harper's appetite for dinner, what should we fix?"

"I'm picking up a party tray for our guests tomorrow morning."

"That's tomorrow. What about tonight?" Marc asked.

"What about just ordering a pizza? We'll have lots of leftovers tomorrow and I don't want to cook tonight. Sounds like you don't either."

"We just have to agree on what we want on it."

"I vote for a veggie pizza."

"And I want meat lover's," Marc said.

"I'll call about a half and half. The pizza place is going to question whether a meat lover and a veggie couple can remain married."

"Why would you say that?"

"What do you mean? Don't you get it? Meat lovers. Veggie pizza. Opposites."

"I don't like you implying we wouldn't stay together. Especially over a pizza."

Ravyn was surprised their conversation had taken this turn. Was Marc angry about the pizza or that she'd brought up a subject he'd already been considering?

"Well fine," she said, suddenly angry. "Just order the entire pizza meat lovers. I'll just fix a salad."

"I'm sorry. I'll order the half and half. Should we open a bottle of wine to go with the pizza?" when Marc asked, trying to calm himself and his wife.

"I think we'd better," Ravyn answered, still angry. "I know I'm going to want a drink tonight."

"I said I'm sorry. Your choice of words just caught me off guard."

"My choice of words? What the hell are you talking about?"

"About us not being married. I don't want to even think about that."

"For Christ's sake, Marc, I was making a joke about the pizza! I'm not talking about us not being married!"

"OK, OK. I'm sorry. It's just we've been, umm, at odds lately."

"Well, I've been unhappy that you haven't been at home as much," she admitted." It makes me worry you don't want to be with me or Harper."

Marc reached out to hug Ravyn. "That's not true. That will never be true. I love you," he said, his voice cracking. "I've just been… It's just, with my father gone…"

Marc began to cry, big gulping sobs. Now Ravyn was hugging him hard. She rubbed his back trying to soothe him.

"Let's sit down," she said, steering him to the couch.

They sat, their arms still wrapped around each other. Marc's breathing became more regular.

"I would really like you to go with me to a marriage counselor, Marc. I think what you are feeling might be a lot of grief. And if you don't want to go with me, please seek out your own counselor. A grief counselor. Your father's death has clearly been hard on you. I don't want to see you this sad and unhappy."

"I'm not a sissy. I don't need a counselor."

"I never said or thought you were a sissy, Marc. You are one of the strongest men I know. I think you are overwhelmed. Your father died, your brother is having addiction problems, your mother is injured. You've got a lot going on. I just don't want me and Harper to be the collateral damage."

"What do you mean collateral damage?"

"You've been shutting us out. And we are the ones who you need most!"

"I do need you. But you've been distant too."

"I have? In what way?" Ravyn asked, curious how she'd been distant.

"Well, you've taken that dog over me, when I didn't want him in this house."

"That's not being distant, Marc. That is being a good person who helps out a family member who can't take care of Blaze right now."

"That family member is my deadbeat brother Bruce. That dog is his mangy mutt."

"That mangy mutt saved me and your daughter from a fire!"

"There was never a fire! You said so yourself!"

"Well, there sure was a lot of smoke. I was scared."

They were back to arguing and Harper began to cry at all the shouting. Ravyn went over to comfort her. She worried that her family was coming the next day to celebrate Harper's birthday, that she and Marc were at odds again. She wondered if she could fake a celebratory mood when she didn't feel it.

Marc took some deep breaths, calming himself down. "Should I order the pizza?"

"Do what you want. I've lost my appetite."

Chapter 12

Marc and Ravyn went to bed without speaking to each other, each angry. When they awoke the next morning, Ravyn mumbled that she was taking Blaze and Harper for their morning walk. Marc said he was going to the gym.

When Ravyn returned home, she loaded Harper into the SUV and went to the grocery store to pick up the party trays for the company coming. She was dreading the day now that she and Marc had argued. Why was he making everything so difficult?

She'd thought they'd had a breakthrough when he admitted his feelings the night before, but then he got defensive and mad.

Ravyn felt like she couldn't do or say anything right. She was looking forward to her counseling session. She was sure she would be unloading on all that Marc did wrong. She just hoped the counselor was sympathetic to her plight.

Ravyn's family arrived around noon, and she put on a brave face. Mostly her family wanted to fuss over Harper.

But Julie couldn't be fooled. "What's going on?"

"Marc and I had a big fight last night. Over pizza for God's sake! I made what I thought was a funny comment and he went all crazy. I swear I feel like I'm walking on eggshells around him. I even asked him again to go to counseling with me. He just got madder."

"I'm so sorry. But you are still going to go, right?"

"Yes. I just hope your therapist lets me unload on Marc and takes my side," Ravyn said with a wan smile.

Julie hugged Ravyn. "You are holding up remarkably well."

"Remember me at the Oscars," Ravyn replied, wiping away a quick tear.

"Well, I'm here for you."

"Thank you, Julie. I don't know what I'd do without you."

"You'll never have to find that out. And Ravyn, I couldn't have survived my divorce without you either."

The friends just hugged each other tighter in the kitchen as the party got louder around them.

"Did I tell you I'm taking the test for my real estate license next month?"

"You didn't."

"I'm nervous. Some of the agents in the office have said they didn't pass the first time. And the license fee isn't cheap. I really need to pass it the first time."

"Is there a lot of studying?"

"Yes. And I can't study until the girls are in bed, really. And when Rob has them on the weekends. Then the apartment is quiet, and I can concentrate. There's a lot to learn and remember."

"I'm so proud of you. I just know you will be successful."

"I haven't forgotten about your freelance story. I've gotten the interviews done. I plan to write it this week and turn it in ahead of the deadline."

"You are a godsend! I wish my other freelancers would do the same."

Ravyn's mother Kaye came into the kitchen, interrupting Julie and Ravyn. "There you are! We're about to sing Happy Birthday to Harper."

Ravyn and Julie came out into the living room, where the other family members were gathered. Ravyn and Julie stood near the fireplace that had not been used since the fire.

Marc was across the room near Ravyn's sister Jane and Jane's husband Nick. Their son Connor, just two months older than Harper, was toddling and saying more words.

Connor walked around the living room with one of Harper's stuffed lions, reaching up to give it to Harper, who was in her high chair.

Ravyn had kept Blaze in the backyard, tied up on his leash, away from the guests. She didn't want him getting underfoot, nor getting into the trays of food. She checked on him periodically throughout the afternoon.

By the time everyone left in the early evening, Ravyn was exhausted, with the activity of the party and having to pretend she was having a good time.

After the guests left, her parents and Jane and her family headed back to South Carolina, and Julie and her girls went back to their apartment, Marc turned to her at the front door and said he was leaving too. He was going to visit his mother before visiting hours were over at the hospital.

"Sure. See you later," she said, closing the door behind him.

Honestly, Ravyn was relieved she had the house to herself in peace and quiet.

She brought Blaze back into the house and got Harper into the stroller for a quick walk around the block. It was dark and she put a lighted vest on herself, a blinking light on the stroller, and a lighted harness on Blaze.

When she got back to the house, Harper was asleep. She got her gently into her crib and fed Blaze. Ravyn picked at a few of the leftovers on the party trays, some chicken strips and honey mustard dip, some potato chips and ranch dip, and a few bites of leftover birthday cake.

"Dinner is served," she said to the quiet house. Ravyn then poured a generous glass of wine and sat on the couch. She turned on the TV but quickly got bored. She turned it off, turning on some music instead. She always liked music from the 80s and 90s. Her iTunes was loaded with music from that era.

Blaze came over and jumped on the couch and curled up next to her. Ravyn fell asleep, waking up hours later in a dark house and a sore neck and back. She got up and headed to the bedroom. Marc was not there.

Ravyn got into bed, urging Blaze to get up on the bed with her. She cried herself to sleep holding Blaze tight.

Marc spent a restless night at his mother's house in his childhood bedroom. He'd gone to see her at the hospital and had seen her still in so much pain it worried him. She told him her transfer to the rehabilitation facility was being delayed. No bed was available. Once she was finally admitted, she'd be there for two to four weeks.

Carol told him Bruce was scheduled to be released from his rehab treatment in early March. She begged Marc to look after Bruce at the house since she wouldn't be home yet to care for him. Make sure he ate well and kept out of trouble.

Marc did not want to babysit his brother. Bruce was a grown man who'd made his own bad choices. The words tumbled out of Marc's mouth and his mother began to cry.

Marc felt ashamed. He didn't mean to upset his mother. He certainly didn't mean to make her cry. He could see her push the nurse's call button and ask for some pain medication.

The nurse saw her patient Carol Linder crying and gave Marc a sour look.

"I'm sorry, Mom. I'm sorry. Of course, I'll look after Bruce," Marc said. "It will just be for a few weeks, right?"

Carol nodded. Marc hoped his mother would be home in two weeks, not four. Marc and Bruce would probably kill each other if it was longer.

Marc thought Ravyn was probably going to explode when he told her he'd be at his mother's house for a solid two weeks, or longer, to look after Bruce.

All night Marc tossed and turned, thinking about the liquor he'd have to move to his house, the prescription medicines he'd have to clean out of the bathrooms, and any other items that Bruce might abuse.

Marc got up, unable to settle down. He went to his father's liquor cabinet and pulled out a 12-year-old scotch and a glass from the liquor cabinet. Marc gave a sad smile thinking he learned to drink and like scotch thanks to Edward.

"Thanks, Dad," he whispered, lifting his glass in the air.

Marc sat on a leather chair — his father's chair — in the dark living room and nursed his first few fingers of scotch. Marc could almost picture his father sitting in this exact chair with the crystal low-ball glass filled halfway with scotch. A similar glass that Marc now held in his hand.

Marc pulled his hand through his hair and then across his stubbled chin. He should have called Ravyn that night to at least say good night and let her know he wasn't going to be home.

He was just so angry. With himself, with Ravyn, with the situation he now found himself in with Bruce, his late father, and his injured mother.

Marc felt himself drowning in responsibility. He felt a wave of unnatural anger toward Bruce's dog, as well. Why was his family forced to take care of it? He should have insisted Ravyn take the dog to an animal shelter and find a good adoptive home for it.

He really didn't want Ravyn to get too attached to the dog. He didn't want Harper to get attached to it either. My God! Harper was saying the dog's name!

Marc half smiled in the dark. Harper was cute when she tried to say Blaze's name. Baas.

Marc poured another few fingers of scotch. He would be sure this bottle ended up at his house.

He remembered the first time he'd found his brother Bruce drunk. Bruce had been a freshman or sophomore in high school. Bruce had gotten into his father's liquor cabinet and drank some very expensive whiskey.

Marc had come home from college one Friday afternoon to find Bruce had puked on the carpet and passed out. Marc got him on his feet and got him into the shower. He turned the water on while Bruce was still fully clothed. Marc tried to breathe through his mouth to keep from being sick himself.

Marc grabbed some towels and tried to clean up the vomit, but it was really no use. He wasn't going to be able to cover for his brother on this one. Nor did he want to. Bruce had been acting so erratic, failing classes, skipping school. His mother had told him so.

Like an epiphany, Marc realized that must have been around the time in Bruce's life when he had been assaulted. He'd have been — what? Fourteen?

Six years older than his brother, Marc was attending the University of Georgia by then, studying pre-law to follow in his father's footsteps. Marc's mother had told him his brother had been acting strange, out of character. The fuzzy memories of half a lifetime ago became clearer.

Marc gulped down the remainder of his scotch, feeling the liquid burn as it went down his throat, then feeling it sour in his stomach. He wanted to hurl the crystal low ball glass through the front door's decorative plate glass window.

Having had to postpone their girls' dinner with all the commotion going on in their lives, Ravyn drove to Julie's apartment with Harper a week after Harper's birthday.

Julie's girls were going to watch Harper in the 90 minutes the women were at Seven Lamps. Ashley was excited it was her first real babysitting job.

Julie told both girls to call if anything went wrong. Julie could see the look of worry on Ravyn's face but knew they both needed this dinner.

After they ordered their cocktails, they looked over the menu and ordered an appetizer then ordered their meals.

"OK, I'm here to listen," Ravyn said. "What is going on with that skank?"

"It's really just awful. I told you she's pregnant and that it's a boy. My girls are excited about a baby brother. My life is over."

"Your life is not over. I know this is a blow, but your life is not over."

"Well, I am studying for my real estate license. I'm excited about that. And I'm grateful I can study at the real estate office. The employees there are so kind when I ask questions. I was hoping to have a few more jobs staging homes, but it's slowed down a bit. My friend keeps telling me to hold on; it will be very busy in about a month. Spring season."

"Spring season?"

"People put their homes on the market in the spring so they can move during the summer, so they don't have to put their kids in a new school before the end of the school year."

"Are you thinking of finding a place?"

"No. I'm locked into my lease until the end of the year. Plus, the girls' tennis lessons are about to start, and the apartment isn't far from the courts."

"Sounds like you are starting to settle in there."

"I'm not hating it as much. It's small and the girls can drive me insane. They hate sharing a bathroom. I am really looking forward to when the pool opens in May. You and Harper will have to come over."

"Oh my God! I forgot to tell you Harper took her first steps!"

"She did? That's wonderful."

"I'm glad Marc was at the house with me. We both saw her. She stood up and took a few steps toward the stroller. She knew we were going for a walk with Blaze. She even tried to say 'Blaze.' It came out as 'baas.' It was cute."

"You are keeping the dog?"

"Well, I have no real problem with him. Now that I've gotten rid of the fleas, gotten him on heartworm medicine, and given him better dog food so he doesn't fart as much, I feel pretty invested in him. And he did alert me to the fire in the chimney."

"I feel like there's a 'but' about to come with this story."

"But Blaze is Bruce's dog and Marc is pretty angry at Bruce these days. He's pretty mad at everything these days."

"Sounds like he needs some therapy."

"I've suggested it on numerous occasions, and it never goes over well. And I had to postpone my initial consultation with your therapist until next week. I'm really looking forward to it."

"Postpone? Why?"

"Her office called and said she had a family emergency, so she actually rescheduled it. I'm glad it wasn't canceled altogether."

"I'm glad you are going. I think you will really like her."

"I really just want to unload. I hope I don't get too weepy."

"I think she buys tissues by the truckload."

Ravyn burst out laughing. The waiter came over to see if their meal was OK and asked if they wanted another cocktail.

"We better not," Julie said. "We have to get home."

When the waiter left to bring their check, Julie said, "I'm concerned about all this anger from Marc, especially toward you."

"I'll be honest, Julie. Things have really changed between us. Ever since his father died. And I can't exactly tell him to neglect his widowed mother. Especially now that she's fallen and broken her hip for God's sake. I'll come off like a shrew."

"I don't think you are acting like a shrew. I think you are a wife who is frustrated by the situation."

"He pursued me, Julie. Now that he has me, well…"

"I really hope my therapist can help you," Julie said as she reached across the table and held Ravyn's hand. "Give you some good advice and coping skills."

"I do too," she said, giving Julie's hand a squeeze.

Chapter 13

Marc got up at 4:30 a.m., unable to sleep. He decided he'd just go to the gym. He was thankful he still had some gym shorts and an old T-shirt in a drawer of his old room.

He put on a sweatshirt against the chill of the February morning and headed to the Dunwoody location of his gym. He was glad he'd gotten a membership so he could go to any location in the United States.

This wasn't his normal gym, so he didn't think there would be a boxing class that he liked, but he did work the heavy bag for a half hour. Marc worked up a sweat, getting out his frustration and aggression on the bag, then turned to the speed bag, working on his punches and jabs.

Marc realized he'd gathered a small crowd who watched him work out with interest.

"Hey!" called out one gym member. "Haven't seen you here before. You new here?"

"I'm staying at my parent's house temporarily, so I came here today to work out."

"You're good. You have good hands. Have you ever thought about stepping into the ring?"

"Well, not really. My wife would kill me if I got hurt."

"I'm Brent," the member said, introducing himself.

"Marc."

With a boxing glove on, the only thing they could do was fist bump each other.

"Do you get in the ring often?" Marc asked, taking off his gloves.

"Yes. The first time, I got my ass handed to me," Brent said, smiling at the memory.

"I'd like to see you fight some time."

"Let me give you my number. Text me and I can let you know my next match. Maybe I can convince you to come fight some time."

"Maybe," Marc said.

Marc showered and headed back to his Buckhead home. He figured he'd better tell Ravyn in person about the upcoming change in his living arrangements.

He walked into his home and heard silence. He walked into Harper's room and found her still asleep on her back with Felix curled up next to her. He walked into the master bedroom and found Ravyn curled up in bed with Blaze. He frowned at that. He didn't want that dog in his bed. He felt itchy just thinking about it.

Blaze looked up as Marc stood at the door. Marc could almost feel the dog's hostility toward him.

"Yeah. I don't like you either," Marc said under his breath.

Blaze gave a little "woof" and Ravyn stirred, rolling over toward the door. She realized Marc was in the doorway and sat up with a start.

"I didn't hear you come in," she said, yawning and reaching for her phone. "What time is it?"

"Not quite seven," he said. "Listen, I'll make coffee. We need to talk."

Ravyn's heart started beating rapidly. "Talk?"

"About my mother's care. Come into the kitchen."

Ravyn pulled on her robe and followed Marc into the kitchen. He reached for the coffee and got the coffee maker started.

"Sit," he said, gesturing to a chair at the breakfast table.

"I feel like you are going to give me bad news," she said, worried.

Marc sighed. "It's not great news. My mother is being transferred to the rehab facility this Wednesday."

"That's great news. Why is it not great news?"

"She'll be there from two to four weeks."

"But she'll be in good care, right?"

"Yes. She'll get the care she needs to begin physical therapy and walking again."

"Then what's wrong?"

"Bruce gets out of rehab in less than a week," Marc said, frowning.

"So?"

"He's coming back to my mother's house. And she won't be there to care for him. Keep an eye out on him, really."

"Oh."

"My mother made me promise I'd live with him and take care of him until she is released from the rehab facility." Marc looked so serious, but his words caught Ravyn off guard.

"What?"

"I promised her."

"What about us?"

Marc's face brightened. "Why don't you come live in the house with us? Why didn't I think of this before? You can just move into the Dunwoody house until my mother gets home."

"Marc, my commute will be even worse. I do not want to commute on 285. And what about Blaze? You said your mother is allergic. We can't all move in."

"That fucking dog," Marc scowled. "I should have dropped him off at the pound when you first brought him into this house."

As if Blaze had understood every word Marc said, Blaze began a low growl at Marc.

"You know that dog hates me," he said, flatly.

"You've never given him any reason to believe you like him. Dogs are sensitive to feelings, Marc."

"That dog isn't sensitive to my feelings. He's just a dog, and a mutt at that."

"He is NOT just a dog, Marc. He's a good boy. He's needed a little work. Bruce didn't exactly train him."

"Train him! That's a good joke. You'd need to train Bruce first!"

"Marc, that's unkind. And since Bruce found Blaze as a stray, he's likely been on his own for a while. But he's a quick learner. I've got him leash trained now and he's a good dog to take running. I feel safer with him on our early morning runs."

"I'm glad he's there with you, then. I still wish I'd taken him to the pound."

"I'm not. It's not like you to harm an animal. Why do you dislike Blaze so much?"

"Because he reminds me too much of Bruce. Homeless, ill-mannered, a loser."

"Blaze and Bruce are none of those things, Marc. And you know that."

Marc knit his brow and changed the subject. "You are right about Blaze. I can't bring him into my mother's home. I wish I didn't have to let Bruce into my mother's home, either."

"When does Bruce get out of rehab? The exact day? You can live here until that happens, right?" Ravyn asked, excited that Marc would finally be home for a little while.

"I'll call tomorrow and find out what day he'll be released. Mother was vague about it. She probably didn't know the exact day either."

"But you'll spend today here?"

"Of course. Where else would I go?"

"Nowhere else. Stay with me," she said, as she wrapped her arms around her husband.

Ravyn awoke for the second time that morning, only this time in Marc's arms. She could hear Harper babbling on the baby monitor. Blaze wasn't in the master bedroom, so she assumed Blaze was keeping her company. Then she heard an all too familiar word from Harper these days: "Baas."

She imagined Felix was also curled up in Harper's crib. Ever since Felix had landed a large scratch on Blaze's nose, they'd declared a truce.

Ravyn snuggled closer to Marc. She could hear him softly snoring.

They'd barely had a cup of coffee earlier that morning and then had headed back to bed and made love. She was happy. Ravyn felt as if, as a couple, they were getting back on track.

"Wake up, sleepy head," Ravyn teased, running her hand along Marc's lean stomach. She was tempted to reach down lower but thought that Harper, Felix, and Blaze would protest their hunger.

Marc stretched and rubbed his eyes, then his whiskered chin. "But I don't want to get up. I want to stay all day in bed with you."

"Oh, the days before we had a child, and we could do that. Now we have a child and a dog that need some attention. Why don't you come on a walk with me, Harper, and Blaze? Maybe he'll get a little more used to you if you interact with him."

"I really don't want to interact with that dog."

"Come on, Marc," Ravyn said, swatting his arm.

"Oww."

"What do you mean, oww? I didn't hit you that hard."

"I couldn't sleep last night so I got up and went to the gym near my mother's house. I worked on the heavy bag and my arms are sore now."

"Why couldn't you sleep?"

"Worried about when Bruce comes home. I've got to clear out all the liquor and any prescriptions, or anything he might abuse, from the house. I don't want any temptations there."

"What are you going to do with it? Dump it out? Have one spectacular party like in one of those teenage movies?"

"Hell no. My father had top-shelf liquor. I'll bring it all here."

"Won't your mother be angry when all the alcohol is gone from her house? She likes a cocktail now and again. When she gets home, she'll probably be ready for one."

"Well, when she gets out of her facility, I'll bring most of it back. She likes her gin and tonics and dry martinis. I can bring those liquors back."

"But she doesn't expect you to stay in the house with Bruce 24/7, does she? How will you work?"

"I think that's exactly what she's expecting. I think she would have done it if she hadn't fallen."

"Marc, that's a lot to ask."

"I promised her," Marc said softly. "And I made her cry."

"You made her cry?"

"I said something — unkind, as you put it — about Bruce."

"Ah. She guilted you into staying at the house."

"And now you are beginning to understand my mother. She can lay down quite the guilt trip. I guess I can go to work when Bruce goes to work, but I have no idea what his schedule is. I don't think he works a 9-to-5 job. I think he works different shifts."

Marc sighed and rubbed his chin.

"If you want to sleep some more, I'll take care of Harper and Blaze."

"No, I'll get up, too."

Ravyn got up, fed Harper a quick bowl of hot cereal, and gave Blaze a small portion of food. She didn't want him to be sick on their run. Next, she got Harper in some warm clothes, and she put on her running gear. It was still cool enough that morning for long sleeves and her capris.

Harper was standing by the stroller, holding on with one hand while Blaze licked her face. "No, Baas." She was waving her arm at him to make him stop.

Ravyn wished she had her camera. They looked so cute together.

"Come on, gang. Let's go!" Ravyn lifted Harper into her stroller.

Harper pointed her finger forward and kicked her feet.

Ravyn gathered the leash and the trio hit the neighborhood streets.

When Ravyn returned, Marc was cooking bacon and was about to make omelets for a late breakfast. Ravyn's mouth watered at the smells.

"Dada," Harper said, pointing to Marc.

"Dada fixed us some more yummy breakfast. Mmm," Ravyn said, rubbing her tummy.

Harper mimicked what Ravyn was doing, parroting "Mmm."

"Do you want an omelet, too, or how about some scrambled eggs?" Marc asked her.

Harper just pointed her finger in his direction. "Dada."

Blaze stood behind Marc, sniffing the air.

"I think Blaze would like whatever you are making, too."

"That mutt, I mean Blaze, will not be having any omelet today. Doesn't he have dog food? As I remember, you were buying the expensive kind for him."

"Well, that stuff Bruce had wasn't good for him. Must have been the cheapest stuff out there. With his new food, he has a shiny coat and better poops."

"That's appetizing."

"You didn't have to clean up the unappetizing results of that crappy food. No pun intended. I'm just thrilled to be picking up anything solid now."

Marc made a face at Ravyn. "Can we change the subject? Or I'm not going to be able to eat my breakfast."

"Well, he is doing a lot better."

"What happens when Bruce goes back to his apartment and wants him back? What then? You shouldn't get too attached to him. He's not your dog, Ravyn."

Marc looked back at Ravyn while he stirred the eggs. He thought she was going to cry.

"I'm sorry. I didn't mean to…"

"I know he's not my dog! But I can still care about his health and well-being!" Ravyn exclaimed.

"Of course. Of course, you do," Marc said, stopping what he was doing and hugging his wife. "You keep him healthy and happy until we can bring him back to Bruce's care."

"I'm just trying to do the right thing."

"I know you are, and I love you for it. I promise I'll try not to be so angry about the dog. I guess I'm really just angry at my brother."

"Why are you so angry at him?"

"What I'm about to tell you is in confidence. Bruce didn't tell me. Brooke did," Marc said. He paused and took a deep breath. "Bruce was sexually assaulted when he was a kid. It's why he's had so many *issues*."

"Oh, I know about that."

"You knew?!" Marc asked, astonished.

"Bruce told me."

"He told you and he never confided in me? Why didn't you tell me?"

"Marc, that is news only he can tell you. That's not news for me to tell you."

Marc was angry again. He pulled his hand through his hair.

"I just can't believe he told everyone but me!"

"He didn't tell your father, either. Said your father would never understand."

"And I wouldn't? Does he think I'm as insensitive as my father?"

"Marc, I think he was worried about your reaction. It was a traumatic event and Bruce is far more sensitive than you are."

"I'm not sensitive? What the hell?"

"I mean you have a very different personality than Bruce. You are confident and more outspoken. Bruce is quieter and more sensitive than you are. And based on the reaction you are having now, I can see why he didn't take you in his confidence."

"I can't believe you think I'm an insensitive asshole."

"I did not say that."

"Well, I just thought you would be on my side."

"I *am* on your side. I will always *be* on your side."

"It doesn't feel like it."

"I wish you would change your mind about coming with me to marriage counseling."

"I don't need a therapist. I don't think you do either. It's a waste of money. Especially if you go to Julie's therapist. Julie should demand her money back."

"Marc, that is a terrible thing to say! I'm not sure the therapist was at fault if Rob couldn't keep it in his pants. Now, are you fixing those omelets because I'm famished."

"You are changing the subject."

"I'm changing the subject because I'm hungry and I was promised omelets."

Marc turned back to the omelet pan and began to make breakfast in silence.

"Don't be mad at me. I really am hungry."

Marc made the omelet for Ravyn, put it on the plate and put it in front of her without saying a word. He scrambled some eggs for Harper and put them on a small plastic plate and put that in front of her in the high chair. He then flipped a piece of bacon at Blaze, who caught it in mid-air.

Marc then walked back to the bedroom.

Chapter 14

For the rest of that Sunday, Ravyn was on pins and needles with Marc, who turned moody and distant. They went to bed in silence and didn't cuddle. Ravyn found it hard to sleep next to Marc without touching him. She felt like she was a mannequin.

Ravyn was relieved when she found Marc still in the bed Monday morning. She was hoping he would take Harper to daycare that morning, giving her a break to just run with Blaze during their morning routine.

Marc gave an abrupt goodbye as he loaded Harper in her car seat before leaving that morning.

Ravyn felt like she was back at square one with Marc. She was looking forward to her therapy session next week. She had a lot of unloading to do. She hoped the therapist had a lot of facial tissues.

Ravyn got to her office and got settled in. She was behind in her work and stayed focused all morning, not even looking up until it was almost one o'clock.

Gavin Owens, the photographer, stuck his head in her office door, knocking lightly as he did so.

"Hey, do you have a minute?"

Ravyn looked up and smiled. "Of course. What do you need?"

"We haven't talked about the cover for the May issue."

"Oh my God! We haven't!"

Working at a magazine, Ravyn was always working two months ahead on issues, so the upcoming issue was for May. She had a cover story but had neglected to talk to Gavin about cover ideas for the magazine. She knew he had already shot the cover story.

"Was there anything that stood out, art wise, in the cover story?"

"Ah, not really. That's why we need to talk."

"Well, crap. I was hoping you shot something inspired that would work for the cover."

The cover story was about summer getaways. Metro Atlanta schools got out around Memorial Day and a summer getaways feature, which was published in late April, would make readers think about where they wanted to escape on vacation.

"I really don't want to use a stock photo for the cover," Ravyn said.

"The problem is, of course, it's still February and everything I've shot looks like winter. Brown grass, gray skies. I think Chase would kill me if I asked him to photoshop the entire photo to create green grass and blue skies."

"I mean I could ask for stock photos of some of the resorts. They'll have all that stuff, and I'm sure it was shot in summer. We could go with a collage cover. But are you OK with that? It won't be your work."

"I guess I'm going to have to be OK with it."

"I'm sorry, Gavin. I should have asked you to shoot some of these things last year."

"Well, you didn't know."

"Not really. We've moved the editorial calendar around so much."

The editorial calendar was a mix of stories that the advertising staff thought they could sell. Sometimes, the stories got shifted if the ad staff believed they could sell ads for that issue.

"Tell me about it. Chase is about to tear his hair out about the June issue."

Ravyn shook her head. Chase Riley, the art director, was already thinking about the June issue, which was all about in-home and public pools, where many Atlantans got memberships. Except public pools wouldn't open until late May. Hard to illustrate when it was still cold out and pools were closed.

Ravyn had originally pitched a tennis cover story idea. She knew from Julie tennis was played nearly all year round. They could get photos on tennis courts easily.

But Joel Greenburg, the advertising director, insisted on switching out the June issue to pools, thinking he could get lots of independent pool cleaners, installers, suppliers, and pool clubs to advertise for the issue.

That left Ravyn to switch up her cover stories and ideas for the next two issues. But right now, she needed to finish the April issue of *Cleopatra*.

"OK, if you are alright with a cover collage, I'll go ahead and email the resorts in the story for some stock art."

"Hey, I think we are trying to have another pizza party. Nathan in design is getting married."

"I hadn't heard that. Well, I'll have to congratulate him. When is the party? I hope I can go. My home life is a little crazy these days and if it's not in the next two weeks, I probably can't come."

"What's going on?"

Ravyn was silent.

"I'm sorry, you don't have to tell me if you don't want to."

"It's no secret my father-in-law died."

"I was sorry to hear about your loss."

"Thank you. It's hitting my husband pretty hard. And then his mother fell and broke her hip."

"Oh, God. I didn't hear that. Is she OK?"

"Well, she's getting out of the hospital soon, and will go into a rehabilitation facility to get physical therapy and all that. My husband has been spending a lot of time away from home, which means I've been a bit of a single mother."

"Oh, sorry. That must be rough."

"Honestly, it's why I'm behind on all my assignments. It has been rough. But hopefully, it will be temporary. His mother will heal. I just hope it is sooner rather than later."

"I'll pray for you and your family," Gavin said, earnestly.

Ravyn didn't realize he was so religious but accepted the prayers. Goodness knows she needed them to help her get through what was happening at home and when Marc was going to be at his mother's house with Bruce.

Suddenly she thought of Marc and Bruce together. She did not envision it would go well.

"Gavin, can you keep my family in your prayers for a few weeks? We're going to need it."

"Of course. Do you want me to ask my church to pray for you?"

"That would be great. I'd appreciate it."

Ravyn drove through Atlanta traffic headed to Colony Square to pick up her daughter.

Normally, she and Marc texted constantly throughout the day, but today she heard nothing from him. She expected he was still mad from Sunday. Why was he so touchy these days?

She got Harper and headed for home. She was hoping she got home before Marc and could just get a run in with Blaze and Harper.

When they were out on their run, Ravyn thought about what Marc had said. Blaze was not their dog. She shouldn't get too attached. But she realized it was too late for that.

She loved that dog. He was a quirky dog, yes. But he clearly was protective of her and Harper. And, miracle of miracles, he now got along with Felix. Or at least, if they didn't exactly get along, there was a detente.

How could Ravyn let him go? Could she get another dog for Bruce? Would that be the answer? Maybe not. She realized it would break her heart to part with Blaze. She thought he was a great dog. A really good boy.

Ravyn had worked with him, though. Blaze just needed some guidance and training. He was running well on the leash. In fact, he loved to run. And that helped calm him down. With the food she'd gotten him, he was healthier and happier, she thought.

She'd gotten the fleas under control and gotten him on heartworm medicine. All in all, he was a great dog. She didn't want to give him up.

Ravyn shook her head on the run. She'd have to think about that when the time came. And she didn't want to think about it now, or ever.

When she got home, she realized she'd gotten a text from Marc. He was going to go to the gym.

Ravyn was tired of her husband practically shunning his own family. She and Harper needed him too. She was going to pour herself a big glass of wine tonight.

The house was quiet when Ravyn finally sat down on the couch with her glass of red wine.

Harper was asleep in her crib. Felix was curled up next to her. Blaze joined Ravyn on the couch. She took a sip of her wine, and felt her stomach do a little flip.

Ravyn took a deep breath to calm herself. With everything going on in her life, she just thought what she was feeling was stress.

She took another sip of the wine, but still felt a little funny in her stomach. She put the glass back on the end table. She rubbed Blaze's fur.

Ravyn began to worry she was pregnant again. She'd meant to call the doctor about going back on the pill, but she'd forgotten. And she and Marc had made love, but with no protection.

No way, she thought. I took that pregnancy test, and it was negative. I am *not* pregnant.

She picked up her wine glass and took a bigger sip. Her stomach was still a little funny, so she only drank half the glass.

The house seemed too quiet with Marc gone. She wondered if he'd come home tonight or sleep in the Dunwoody house.

"Well, Blaze, I guess we'd better go to bed."

Ravyn got up and Blaze followed her into the master bedroom. He jumped up onto the bed, turned a couple of times, then settled down on Marc's side of the bed. At least Ravyn would sleep next to a warm body tonight.

Ravyn undressed, then put on her flannel pajamas. She lifted the bed sheet and duvet and slid in next to Blaze. She threw her arm around him and fell sound asleep.

"Have I been replaced?" a deep male voice said in the darkness of the bedroom.

Marc's voice startled Ravyn awake, and Blaze began barking.

"Some watchdog. I was in the bedroom before either of you heard me," he said. "Can I turn on the light?"

Ravyn shielded her eyes before saying yes.

"Come on, Blaze," Marc commanded. "Out. Go check on Harper."

Marc shut the door behind Blaze as the dog padded out into the hallway with just an annoyed woof. Then Marc undressed and got ready for bed.

"I didn't think you were coming home tonight. You said you were going to the gym but then it got late. I thought maybe you'd stay at the Dunwoody house."

"I was there. Did you want me to stay at my mother's house?"

"Of course not. I would have stayed up if I'd known you would be here."

"It's after midnight."

"Oh. Did you go back to the hospital?"

"I did go to the hospital, then I went by the house to get some things my mother requested. I have no idea why she wants her makeup and moisturizers. It's not like anyone but me is going to be visiting her at the rehab facility."

"Marc, she just wants to be presentable, no matter who the visitor is. It will make her feel feminine, like her old self."

"It took me a while to find all of her stuff. She even gave me a list. I had to leave the stuff in a bag at the front desk since hospital visiting hours were over. They said they'd put it in her room when they checked on her later. She's going to need a suitcase for all her things. I didn't even get the clothes she asked for. I'll do that tomorrow."

"I'm glad you are here. Blaze smells better than he did, but he still smells like a dog, with dog breath. You smell much better. Slightly spicy."

"Slightly spicy, huh? That's some sexy talk. At least you didn't accuse me of having dog breath, too."

"Maybe in the morning."

Marc chuckled, turned out the light and got into bed next to Ravyn. "You have too many clothes on."

"Do I? What are you going to do about it?"

"I'm going to remove them one by one. Like strip poker only without the cards. And you, my love, are holding the losing hand."

"Now who's talking sexy?"

Ravyn felt Marc's hand under her flannel nightshirt, cupping her breast. "This comes off first," he said, pulling the shirt over her head. Ravyn put her arms up so he could remove it easily. "Next, these come off," he said, pulling at the waistband of her pajama bottoms.

Those were a little more difficult to pull off under the covers, but at last, they were at her ankles, and she kicked them off.

Ravyn could feel Marc's stiff dick on her thigh. It turned her on. She could feel herself getting wet. Ravyn ached to feel Marc inside her.

They made love slowly, Marc teasing her with his tongue, licking her nipples. Ravyn stroked his shaft, running her thumb over its head.

Marc and Ravyn groaned together before Marc entered her. He held back until Ravyn began to orgasm, then he let his orgasm release.

Marc collapsed to her side. They were both sweaty and spent. "I love you, Marc," Ravyn whispered.

"I love you more," he replied.

Marc's alarm went off first, and Ravyn stretched, then burrowed under the duvet.

"I wish we didn't have to go to work today," she mumbled.

"Kyle wants a meeting today, so I'll have to be in the office, too."

"Is he back in Atlanta?"

"It's a conference call, but I think he will be in Atlanta tomorrow. He's invested in a couple of more local businesses here. I'm sure he'll come to the Atlanta office at some point soon and I'd better be ready."

"Ready?"

"It's late February and with all that's gone on with my dad's death, I haven't made second quarter projections. I'm sure he'll ask about it this morning."

"Surely he understands you've had a death in your immediate family. He'll cut you some slack, won't he?"

"Ravyn, he's an investor. He wants numbers, no matter who died. Unless it's me."

"Don't even say that!"

"It's true, unfortunately."

"That sounds a little harsh."

"He did give me more bereavement time than a regular employee would have gotten. But I had so much to do with the funeral and all that, and then when my mother fell. I am not looking forward to telling him I'll need more time off if I have to babysit Bruce."

"Do you know when Bruce is being released?"

"I meant to call today, but honestly, I wish he'd just stay there until my mother gets out of rehab. Then he can take care of her at the house, and I won't have to get involved."

"If he's ready to be released, he's ready to be released. He's not a prisoner there. And didn't you say he was on a work release program? Surely, he'll still go to work during the week so you can go to work, too."

"Yes, he is on work release, but I don't know what his schedule is. I might have to be with him on his off days."

"Oh. I was hoping you'd only have to be there in the evenings and at night during the work week. I didn't think about him working on the weekends. Maybe he could stay here. Did you think of that? We all could look out for him."

"I don't think that's such a good idea, Ravyn, especially if I bring all the liquor here. I don't want him to be tempted. I think it would be best if I stay with him at the house."

"I won't get to see you at all during that time."

"We'll work something out. You can come up to Dunwoody with Harper and have dinner several times during the week."

"Gee, thanks."

"It's not that I don't want to see you. I just don't know what kind of shape Bruce will be in once he gets out of rehab."

"Marc, it isn't jail. It's not like he's coming out a hardened criminal."

"You just don't know him, Ravyn. I know I keep saying that, but you really don't. You've only seen the sober side of him. When he's somewhat dependable and not having meltdowns. I've seen a very different side of him. A man who gets violent when he's strung out. I don't want that Bruce around my family. I can't take that chance."

Ravyn was silent.

"I just wish all this was different."

"I do too. Honestly, I'm not looking forward to it. Especially now that I know what happened to Bruce. What am I supposed to say? That I don't know?"

"Marc, you have to let him tell you. It's his story to tell. You can't force him. It will make things worse."

"How much worse can it be?"

"Marc, when it comes to sexual trauma, it can get much worse."

Marc was silent and looked at Ravyn. "It sounds like you speak from experience," he said softly.

"No, no. It's not like that. Well, it wasn't that bad for me. I wasn't raped."

Marc now looked at Ravyn alarmed. "What are you talking about?"

"Marc, I was in college and was mooning over a guy. Really crazy about him. He was on the swim team and had a really great body."

Marc scowled. "And?"

"And he invited me up to his frat room. He told me it was to listen to some music. Can you believe I fell for that bullshit? Seriously. It was bullshit."

"What happened?"

"We sat down on his bed, and he began to make the moves on me, putting his hands up my shirt, feeling me up. Now remember, we were not dating. We were not a couple. I just thought he was super cute. And then he went a little too far."

"Too far?"

Ravyn looked away from Marc as she remembered the rest of the story.

"He pushed me down on the bed. He was strong and I'm sure it would have been rape if another frat member hadn't accidentally opened his bedroom door. It startled Mike and I screamed. I got up and ran out the door, never looking back."

"Oh Ravyn, I'm so sorry," Marc said, hugging her to him.

"It's kind of why the 'Me too' movement has been hard for me. I know exactly how those women feel, and nothing really happened to me thanks to that drunk frat brother who opened the wrong door."

"Thank God he did."

Suddenly Ravyn was overcome with emotion and began crying. "I've never told that story to anyone. Not even Julie."

"I'm glad you shared it with me. And if I ever meet up with Mike, whatever his name is, I'll kill him."

"I do not need you to end up in jail for me. I think telling me you'll break his kneecaps will do."

Marc and Ravyn laughed, although hers were through her tears. Why was she so weepy these days?

In her head, she thought she needed to make an appointment with her doctor to go back on the pill.

Marc and Ravyn's routine returned to normal that week, except for Ravyn's appointment Thursday with the therapist.

Ravyn had told Marc he needed to pick up Harper because she was seeing Dr. Jessica Harrison, the therapist.

"Without me?"

"You wouldn't agree to go with me!"

Ravyn was nervous walking into Dr. Harrison's office. There was a plush leather chair across from her desk. It immediately made Ravyn think of her father-in-law's chair.

Jessica shook Ravyn's hand, asking her to call her Jessica.

"What brings you here today, Ravyn?"

Ravyn sat down and said there were a lot of things that brought her to Jessica's office that day.

Before she could even speak, Ravyn began crying, and reached for the box of tissues right near the chair.

"Really I'm not quite sure why I'm so weepy these days. It's just, there's a lot going on in my life and my husband won't come with me to therapy."

Jessica sat silent, waiting for Ravyn to gather herself.

"I want you to understand I love my husband," Ravyn started through her sobs. "But we've had some big challenges lately. I feel we are drifting apart. And he's been so angry lately."

"Do you feel unsafe in your home, because of your husband's anger?" Jessica asked, concerned.

"No, that's not it at all. His father died recently, and I think he's having a lot of trouble dealing with it. Then his mother fell and broke her hip. He hasn't been home a lot."

"Where has he been?"

Ravyn related that Marc had been spending a lot of time at his mother's house following the funeral, taking care of her. With Carol in the hospital, Marc had still been spending time there. Then she told the story of Bruce.

"You will keep that in confidence, won't you? Bruce told me about the assault in confidence."

"Ravyn, everything you tell me today, unless a crime has been committed, is in confidence. If a crime has been committed, I am obligated to tell the authorities."

"No crime has been committed, I swear. I'm just feeling neglected as a new mother and, frankly, overwhelmed. I didn't think I was signing on for all of this when I got married."

Ravyn broke down in tears again.

"Let's talk first about your expectations as a married woman," Jessica said in a soothing voice. "Did you expect your husband would provide for you and your daughter?"

"Yes and no. I work. And I find that my work fulfills me. I certainly didn't want or expect a sugar daddy."

"Are you sure of your feelings? In your initial form, you said your husband Marc makes considerably more than you do. Does that make you feel inferior?"

Ravyn could barely contain her anger at the question. "I do not feel inferior to my husband. I've had to make my own way until we got married."

"Very well. I'm just wanting you to understand your feelings toward your husband. I'm sorry he couldn't join us."

"I begged him to join me."

"And how did he react?"

Ravyn was quiet at first, then said, "He said if you were the marriage counselor for Julie and Rob Montgomery, then you failed. How good could you be?"

"Do you feel that way?"

"I just need someone to talk to and some guidance. I need to know what to do."

"Our time here is almost done so I have some homework for you."

"Homework?"

"Yes, homework. I give my clients homework. Are you ready for it?"

"I guess I am, depending on what it is."

"I think this will be fairly easy for you since you are a journalist and writer. I want you to keep a daily journal of your feelings."

"That's it?"

"I think you will find it harder than you think. You are a working mom, so you will have to make time for it. And your husband may ask what and why you are keeping a journal. He may get defensive about it."

"I think I can do that. I can do it at work, where Marc won't see it."

"I don't want you to keep it secret from him, Ravyn. I want you to tell him about it and tell me about how the homework is going at our next session in three weeks. I find many of my clients can see their emotions more clearly when they are writing them down. Can you do that?"

"Yes. And thank you. I do feel better having talked to you."

"I'm glad. I look forward to our next session."

Chapter 15

Ravyn did tell Marc about her homework assignment from the therapist, but he shrugged at her.

"I'm meeting with her in three weeks. Won't you come with me?"

"No way."

Ravyn felt like Marc could not be persuaded, so she no longer talked to him about it.

The couple continued in their routine until Monday, when it was time for Marc to move into his mother's home to care for Bruce.

Carol had already moved into her rehabilitation center. Marc told Ravyn she wasn't in a private suite. She had another woman in her room, but he was hoping to get her a private room when it became available.

"Do you want me and Harper to come tonight for dinner?" she asked, as Marc readied to begin his two- to three-week stay in Dunwoody.

"No. Let me and Bruce have some time alone tonight. I'm not sure how he will react. Why don't you plan on coming tomorrow night for dinner?"

"OK, if you are sure."

"I'm kind of sure. I wish I knew how this was going to work out."

"Marc, we can't know the future. We can only work on the present."

"Did you read that in a fortune cookie?"

Ravyn's brow creased. Marc was trying to make fun of her. "No. No fortune cookie. Just trying to impart some wisdom."

"Wisdom? Are you sure that's not your therapist talking?"

"You are not even listening, Marc."

"I would listen if you were talking sense."

"Screw you, Marc."

Baby Steps

Marc moved into the Dunwoody house in a sour mood after his fight with Ravyn and awaited Bruce's arrival. Marc found he was nervous and wished he'd not cleared the house of alcohol.

He desperately wanted a scotch. He realized he should have brought his flask with scotch and hidden it in his bedroom. Much like he had done as a teenager in high school.

He'd gotten his alcohol from his father's liquor bar. Marc wondered if his father had ever realized he was missing liquor. He wondered if Bruce had done the same thing as him. How could his father not know if both of his sons were pilfering from the bottles?

On his next trip to his home, Marc planned to fill a couple of flasks with scotch. Did that make him an alcoholic? Marc shook his head. He didn't think so. His brother was the alcoholic in the family.

Around seven o'clock, Marc heard the doorbell ring. He knew Bruce was coming via an Uber ride because Marc had paid for it.

Marc opened the door and stared at his brother. Bruce looked clean shaven and in clean clothes. He didn't look too thin, as he had when he was on drugs. Marc was surprised Bruce looked healthy.

"Come in, come in," Marc said, suddenly embarrassed. "This is your home, too."

"Is it?" Bruce asked.

"Of course it is. Come in," Marc said, opening his arms and trying to welcome Bruce into the house.

Bruce put down his suitcase. The paisley printed suitcase was their mother's suitcase, Mark noted.

"Do you want to put that upstairs?"

"Sure."

Bruce brought his belongings to his bedroom. Marc could hear him walking around upstairs and he wondered what was keeping his brother. Bruce eventually came downstairs.

"Are you hungry? I can grill up some burgers," Marc said.

"Why are you here?"

"Mom asked me to be here."

"To spy on me."

"To look after you, if you need anything."

"I don't need anything from you."

"Well Mom asked me to be here so here I am."

"You don't trust me."

"Hey, you didn't give me a reason to trust you."

"I guess Mom doesn't trust me either."

Bruce looked defeated.

"Look, let's just have some burgers and then we can watch television or something."

"Feels weird to not have Mom and Dad in the house."

"We can visit Mom tomorrow. She'll want to see you."

"I don't have a car. It got impounded after my arrest."

"How did you get to work then?"

"The rehab place had a van. Several of us got dropped off throughout the day."

"Can you get your car back?"

Bruce shrugged. "You were the fancy lawyer. You tell me."

"I wasn't that kind of lawyer. But I can ask a friend if you can get your car back."

"Who's driving Dad's car?"

"No one."

"I'll drive that one then."

"Bruce, that's Dad's Lexus."

"Are you saying he'll be needing it?"

Marc stared at his brother. "That's not even funny."

"I didn't mean it to be funny. But it kind of is," Bruce said, smiling at the thought.

"Do you even have a driver's license now?"

"No, the cop took it when he arrested me. But I went through rehab, and I can get it back. I have to petition the court to get it back. I might need your help."

"I have a couple of friends who are still lawyers. I can give you their numbers."

"Marc, I don't have enough to pay for a lawyer. I barely make over minimum wage at the hospital. I thought you could do it for me, for free."

"I could do it for you? For free? Why would I want to do that? I'm not a lawyer anymore."

"But you were a lawyer. You still know how it works, right?"

"I wasn't a criminal lawyer. I was an IP lawyer."

"IP?"

"Intellectual property. It was how I got interested in starting my own business."

"But you can help me, right?"

"Sure, Bruce, I'll help you get your driver's license back. Until then, no driving Dad's Lexus."

"So how am I going to get around?"

"Uber."

"And who's going to pay for that?"

"I guess Mom. I didn't exactly make out in the will either."

"You didn't get cut out entirely. I did."

"You aren't cut out. Mom's giving you part of her inheritance."

"Because I was cut out of the will," Bruce said, angry.

"Listen, Dad didn't exactly do me any favors either. He let me borrow money to shore up my company, but he made me pay interest on that loan. And that interest was higher than any bank would have charged. I think he was trying to teach me a lesson. I'd already taken out a second mortgage on my house, so I couldn't go back to the bank for more money. He knew I was in a tight spot, and he screwed me over, too."

"The will said you didn't have to pay that back. You got something. I got nothing. Nothing!"

"Bruce, I'd already repaid most of the loan back to him when I sold the majority share of my company to the investor. So really, I got nothing, too."

"He screwed both of us, then."

"Essentially, he did."

"I thought he was just a bastard to me," Bruce said, frowning. "Jesus, I would like a drink," he said, looking around at the bar in the living room. "Where's all the alcohol?"

"Bruce…"

"I know I can't have it. We talk about it in our group sessions. That doesn't mean I don't want one."

"I removed the temptation from this house," Marc said.

"All of it? Where did you put it? Oh, in your house. So, you can have all the nice liquor."

"I'm sure I'll drink some of it."

"You don't trust me to remain sober."

"I'm really hoping you will this time. But I thought it best to remove temptation. And trust me, I'd like a drink now, too. I guess we both have to remain sober tonight."

Bruce frowned again.

"What about those burgers? I guess if I can't drink, I can still enjoy a good burger."

"Now you're talking," Marc said.

When Ravyn got to her office the next morning — late because she had to take Blaze and Harper for a quick morning walk and then drive Harper to daycare — she was surprised she'd missed a call from Julie.

Ravyn booted up her computer then called her best friend.

"Hey, sorry I missed your call. What's up?"

"I failed my test."

"What test?"

"For my real estate license. I failed by two points."

Ravyn could tell Julie was near tears. "I'm so sorry. What did your friend say? The one who is a real estate agent? Is that common for first-timers?"

"She said it's not uncommon, but, of course, *she* didn't fail the first time. Makes me feel like such a loser. Maybe I'm not cut out to be a real estate agent."

"You are not a loser, Julie. You are learning something entirely new. I'm sure I'd fail the test, too. And I still think you will be great at it. Can you retake the test?"

"I can, but there are only four centers in Georgia where I can take the exam. I went to the one in Duluth. If I want to take it again soon, I have to pick another center. I may see if I can take it in Macon. That's at least closer than Savannah."

"Wow. I didn't realize there were so few testing centers."

"That's really why I called you earlier. If I can't book the next test on a day when Rob has the girls, I may need some help with them."

"Of course! I'm happy to pick them up from school or look after them on the weekend. Whatever you need."

"Thanks. It's just driving down to Macon and back will eat up my day."

"Completely understand. And that traffic on Interstate 75 to get to and from Macon…"

"Don't remind me. It's brutal no matter what the time is."

"Let me know what day you are scheduled for. I'm sure I can swing it. Did I tell you Marc is staying at the Dunwoody house for the next few weeks?"

"Why?"

"His mother is now in a rehab facility for her hip and Bruce is now out of his rehab facility for addiction. Marc's mother made him promise to stay at the house with Bruce to keep him out of trouble."

"Why can't you and Harper stay with him in the house? Why are you still in Buckhead?"

"The dog. Marc's mother is allergic to dogs."

"The dog."

"Plus, Marc and I had another big fight last night. I asked him to go to the therapist with me next time. Really, I don't understand why he's being so stubborn. I just don't want to see him right now."

"I'm so sorry. Did you like the therapist?"

"I did like her. I can see why you like her, too."

"I guess you can't force Marc to go with you, but you should still go."

"Oh, I will. I may have to bring Harper with me to the next session."

"No, I'll watch Harper since you are watching my girls for me."

"That would be so wonderful. It's a deal."

"What are friends for if not to have each other's backs?"

"I don't know what I'd do without you, Julie."

"I don't know what I'd do without you, either. You've been a lifesaver lately."

"Same. OK, I'd better get to work. I'm so behind already."

"Have a good day, and I'll call you when I know my next exam date."

The friends said their goodbyes and Ravyn dove into her pile of work. She was surprised when it was five thirty and time to go pick up Harper. She hadn't even eaten lunch that day, although she'd thought about it, but decided to keep working.

Ravyn quickly shut down her computer, grabbed her handbag and jacket and headed for the elevator banks.

She saw Advertising Director Joel Greenberg waiting at the elevators, too.

"Hey Joel," she said.

"Hello yourself. Haven't seen you as much at the office lately."

Ravyn gave Joel a frozen smile. Was he remarking about how little she'd been in the office or that he just hadn't seen her in a while?

"We must keep missing each other," she said, trying to be casual.

"You must be busy with your baby."

"She's one now," Ravyn said, as the elevator doors opened.

"About time for another one, right?" Joel joked.

"Bite your tongue! One is plenty for right now."

Joel laughed. "Suit yourself. My ex-wife and I had our kids close. She said she wanted to be out of diapers in five years."

When they got to the lobby, Ravyn asked, "How many children do you have?"

"Three and I'm about to be a grandpa."

"Congratulations! I am looking forward to no more diapers at my house, too. Have a good evening," she called out as she rushed to her car for the ride back to Colony Square to pick up her daughter. At least tonight she wouldn't be late in picking her up.

What time are you coming for dinner tonight? Marc texted Ravyn.

Ravyn shook her head at the message. What made her husband think she wanted to have dinner with him in Dunwoody after their fight last night. She didn't particularly want to do everything she needed to do at home, including walking Blaze, and then bundle Harper back into the car to drive up to Dunwoody.

At this time in the evening, it could take her an hour to get there. And then Harper would be crabby because she was overly hungry.

She hesitated for just a moment before responding that she'd be staying home. Harper had a slight fever. She was going to feed her and put her to bed early.

Ravyn had never just flat out lied to Marc before, but he wasn't home, and he couldn't take Harper's temperature to check.

Give her a kiss from daddy, was Marc's reply.

Will do.

With no plans to rush to Dunwoody, Ravyn took Blaze and Harper on a longer walk that evening, then got everyone fed.

Ravyn curled up on the couch and pulled out a book she'd been meaning to read. This was going to be a very pleasant night.

"Well, Ravyn and Harper aren't coming for dinner tonight," Marc told Bruce.

"Why not?"

"Ravyn says Harper has a fever. I think that's bullshit, but who knows?"

"Why is it bullshit? Maybe Harper *does* have a fever."

"I think that's Ravyn's code for 'I don't want to come to Dunwoody.'"

"I was hoping they'd come. And bring my dog."

"You know Ravyn can't bring your dog. Mom's allergic to dogs."

"Well, I miss him."

"I just wish she could bring him and leave him with you."

"Why? Doesn't she like him?"

"She loves him. So does Harper. Did you know Harper is saying that dog's name?"

"Harper can talk?"

"Well, she just says things like mama and dada. And Baas. That's what she calls your dog."

Bruce was silent. "Wow," was all he could say, his voice husky.

"Oh no, Bruce. We're giving that dog back when the time comes. I'm tired of dog hair in my house. I've got that damned cat of Ravyn's, and cat hair was bad enough. Now with the dog, it's all over my pants and sweaters."

"Sounds like you don't like animals."

"If Ravyn hadn't already had that cat, I would not have had any animals in my house. Animals are for outside."

"You're not keeping Blaze out in the cold, are you?" Bruce asked, concerned.

"No. Ravyn lets that dog sleep in *my bed*! My bed!"

Marc tried not to see the look of relief on Bruce's face.

"And she's buying him expensive dog food. Seems whatever crap you were feeding him upset his tummy," Marc said, derisively. "She bought him a new leash, a collar with his name on it, and flea and heartworm medicine. That dog, Bruce, is well taken care of, believe me."

"You make it sound like I wasn't taking care of him," Bruce said, defensively. "I was taking care of him. I made sure he ate."

"Ravyn told me the condition of your apartment when she went to pick him up, Bruce. The landlord is going to have to burn that apartment."

"OK, maybe I wasn't taking the best care of Blaze, but I was trying."

"Well then, you weren't trying hard enough then."

"I was!" Bruce shouted.

"I'm not arguing with you about that fucking dog, Bruce," Marc shouted back. "I wish I had brought him to the pound the second Ravyn brought him home."

Bruce angrily grabbed Marc's arm and the two brothers began to grapple with each other. Marc was clearly stronger and heavier than Bruce, but Bruce tried to get the better of Marc.

What Bruce didn't know was Marc had been taking boxing lessons, so knew some defensive moves when Bruce tried to come after him.

Bruce tried to grab both of Marc's arms, but Marc flipped Bruce over and both men crashed to the living room floor.

Marc landed on top of Bruce's back, pinning him to the floor.

"Don't hurt me! Don't hurt me!" Bruce wailed.

"Bruce, Bruce, calm down. I'm not going to hurt you."

"Please don't fuck me again. I'll do anything you want. Just don't fuck me again."

Marc was shocked at Bruce's words and quickly scrambled off his brother, who had curled into a fetal ball.

"Bruce," Marc said softly. "I'm not touching you. I'm not going to hurt you."

But Bruce just began sobbing in a tight ball. Marc had never heard his brother cry so hard. He was at a loss as to what to do for his brother.

Marc went to the kitchen and came back with a glass of cold water. He righted an overturned end table they had knocked over and put the glass on it.

Then he crouched down near Bruce. He put his hand on Bruce's arm, who flinched at being touched. Marc quickly drew his hand away.

Instead, he sat down next to his brother. Bruce's breathing slowly became less labored and more even.

"Bruce, can you tell me what happened?"

"I thought, I thought," Bruce choked out. "I thought you were them."

"Who?"

"The boys who attacked me."

"When?"

141

"When I was at camp."

"When was that?"

"In high school."

"And they attacked you? Who did this?"

Bruce sat up, wiping his face, but he wouldn't look at Marc. "It was that camp Mom and Dad wanted me to go to. That wilderness camp. I was so looking forward to it."

"I remember that. I remember you wanted to go."

"I wish I never had," Bruce said, beginning to cry again. "I wish I'd never gone."

"Can you tell me what happened?"

"Three boys teased me, calling me names. Said I was a fairy. Called me gay."

"I'm sorry."

"You don't understand, Marc," Bruce said, his voice getting high. "You were so strong and big in high school. I wasn't. At first, they were just calling me names, and I tried to avoid them."

"Could you go to a counselor at the camp?"

Bruce turned and looked angrily at Marc.

"One of them was the counselor."

"Oh."

"Then one night they crept into my cabin and pulled me out of bed," Bruce said, closing his eyes, trying not to relive the memory. "They took me out into the woods. Said they were going to take the gay out of me."

Bruce began to sob again. "Two of them held me down, got me on my knees and made me suck the counselor's dick. I threw up. He was mad I'd thrown up on him. Then they held me on the ground by my shoulders and he, he..." Bruce broke off.

"Don't say anymore. I don't need to know more."

"I really want a drink now."

Marc handed Bruce the glass of water. "Sorry, brother, this is the hardest stuff we have in the house."

Bruce wiped his red and puffy eyes again and tried to smile. He took the glass and drank it in three gulps.

"Why didn't you ever tell me?" Marc asked quietly.

"I couldn't tell anyone. No one could know. I was so humiliated." Bruce began to cry again.

"I mean later. Why didn't you tell me later?"

"Would you have believed me? Would you?" Bruce asked, angry again.

"I hope that I would have believed you. You told Mom, you told Brooke. You even told my wife. But you didn't confide in me."

"I didn't think I could. You are so much like Dad, Marc. So judgmental."

"I'm not like Dad."

"Oh yes you are!"

Marc's face darkened. "I am not!"

"You are so much like him you can't even see it."

"Is that why you started drinking, and doing drugs?"

"Of course it is, Marc. I just wanted to forget what had happened. But I couldn't," he said, his voice breaking. "I couldn't."

Marc pressed his lips together. "And Dad certainly had plenty for you to get your hands on." He nodded toward the bar.

"Oh, God. The first time I got drunk I got so sick."

"Was that the weekend I came home from school and found you?"

"Maybe. I don't remember. I drank to forget, remember? Dad's liquor was top shelf. At first it was easy going down, but it was hell coming back up." Bruce gave a sad smile.

"Jesus, if you were drinking Dad's liquor and I was sneaking it, too, I wonder why he never confronted us about it. Surely he knew when the bottles got low."

Bruce shrugged. "I don't think he really cared. He probably thought 'Boys will be boys.' I wonder why he had children. He never really seemed to like us."

"He liked Brooke."

"Yeah, he liked Brooke. He liked you far better than me, that's for sure. You were the golden son."

"I might have had his favor, as long as I was a lawyer following in his footsteps. When I realized I hated it and wanted to do something different, I fell out of favor. Believe me, Bruce, I was on his shit list then, too."

"Welcome to the shit list, brother. Just took you longer to get here."

Bruce began to laugh hysterically. He doubled over and held his sides, gulping for air, unable to stop. Suddenly Marc was laughing just as hard.

Before they knew it, both brothers were holding each other, crying hard.

"I love you, Bruce," Marc whispered, holding Bruce tight. "I know I've been angry with you, but I just didn't know. I didn't understand what you had been through."

"I just wanted a big brother. I wanted to tell you, but I didn't think you'd understand."

"I understand now."

Chapter 16

Marc didn't sleep well the night after he and Bruce argued, fought, and reconciled. Bruce's words bothered him. Was he like his father?

Marc hoped that wasn't true. He didn't want to be like his father. Marc tossed and turned, hearing the words Bruce had said when he thought he was being attacked. When he finally slept, he had dreams of being held down and assaulted.

Marc woke up in a cold sweat. He grimaced when he thought about bringing all the alcohol to his house. Now he woke up wishing he could have a drink. It occurred to him, Bruce probably felt the same way.

Marc finally got up, pulled on his robe, and went downstairs to the kitchen. Here he found Bruce at the kitchen table, drinking a glass of water.

"You couldn't sleep either?" Bruce asked.

"No. And I really wanted a drink tonight."

"Me too," Bruce said, holding up the water glass. "This was all I could find."

"I'm really sorry, Bruce."

"Not your fault. It's not anybody's fault."

"It was those boys' fault. Do you know their names? Could we pursue them criminally?"

"Too late. The counselor is dead."

Marc tried to hide the shock from his face. "How do you know?"

"He was killed in a car accident."

"And the other boys?"

"I have no idea. And I really don't want to know. They know what they did. I hope their conscience eats away at them."

"Will you give me their names? I can track them down."

"And do what, Marc? It's been too many years since it happened. They can't be prosecuted. And it's my word against theirs. I asked my counselors in my group session about that."

"Well, I wish they could be prosecuted."

Bruce shrugged. "I wish I could get my license and my car back."

Marc gave a tired smile. "OK, little brother. We'll work on getting those back."

"Actually, the police can keep my crappy car. I want to drive Dad's car."

Marc laughed. "You know you're going to have to take care of it or Dad will haunt you from his grave."

"I'd like to see him try."

Bruce was quiet for a moment. "I'm really hungry."

"We didn't eat last night. Neither one of us was hungry after that. Want me to whip up some omelets?"

"That sounds good. Can we go have dinner at your house tonight? I'd like to see Blaze. I hope he remembers me."

"Sure. I can call Ravyn and let her know we're coming. Maybe we should bring some takeout, so she doesn't feel like she has to cook."

"I like that idea. I like her, Marc. I'm glad you married her."

Marc smiled sadly. "Well, she's pretty pissed off at me lately."

"Why?"

"She wants me to go to a marriage counselor."

"You're not getting a divorce, are you?" Bruce asked, alarmed.

"No. Not at all. Not if I can help it. She's just been angry that I won't go with her."

"Why won't you go? I've gotten a lot of help from my group sessions. I even go to a sexual assault group session now. Most in the session are women though, but there are a few guys, and we break off into our own group."

"I'm glad you are getting help. I just don't think it is for me."

"Just like Dad."

Marc looked at his brother. "Why would you say that?"

"Did you know Mom was ready to leave Dad?"

"What?"

"She was ready to leave him. Asked him to go to counseling, too. You can guess how he reacted to that."

"But she didn't leave him."

"She didn't. She went to counseling, though. I think that is when she moved into her own bedroom."

"What?"

"Yeah, she moved out of their bedroom."

"I never knew that."

"You were in college. When you came home, I think she let you think they were still a happy loving couple. But they weren't. She never told me, but I'm sure she and Dad fought about me."

"I can't believe this! I feel like my whole family had all these secrets they kept from me."

"What do you expect, Marc? And now you won't go with your wife to counseling. Don't you think your marriage is worth fighting for?"

"Of course, I do. I love my wife, Bruce!"

"Then why are you fighting this?"

Marc was silent, scowling. "Just eat your damn breakfast."

He flipped the omelet onto Bruce's plate and began to make his own.

"This is good. Are you sure you aren't the gay man in this family?" Bruce asked.

"Screw you, Bruce."

"Someone beat you to it."

"I'm sorry. I shouldn't have said that."

"You can say whatever you want. You always have spoken your mind. Just like Dad."

"Well, I shouldn't have said that, given your history."

"I'm actually glad we fought last night and cleared the air."

"I am glad you confided in me. I am sorry it happened to you, but I think I understand why you did what you did."

"You mean become a drunk and an addict?"

"Yes," Marc said, ashamed. "I wish I could turn back time, Bruce. I wish we could go back to the way we were before."

"Before the assault.

"Yes, before the assault. I thought we were pretty close. I enjoyed having a little brother. I remember taking you fishing out at Stone Mountain lake. Do you remember that?"

Bruce's face brightened. "I do remember that! You caught a tree limb. I actually caught the only fish."

Marc laughed. "Yeah. Maybe I wasn't such a good teacher when it came to fishing."

"Oh no! You were. I caught the fish."

"I just wish…"

"I know, Marc. I wished for a lot of things, too. But that wishing led me to drink and take drugs to forget. I'm trying to learn to remember and deal with it. I've been diagnosed with PTSD. I don't think I told you that."

"You didn't, but I should have guessed that based on last night."

"I have flashbacks. It's hard. I'm not going to lie. All night I kept wishing there was alcohol in this house. I could taste it. I guess I should thank you for removing it."

"I was wishing I hadn't. I wanted a drink badly, too."

"If you won't go to counseling with Ravyn, would you ever consider coming to one of my sessions?"

"Why? I'm not an addict."

"I'm not saying you are. Lately, I've been talking with my counselor a lot about grief. About the assault, about my life in general, about Dad's death. That man was a bastard and never loved me. I know that now. It helps me to talk about those feelings with my counselor."

"Can I think about it?"

"Sure, Marc," he answered. "My next meeting is Thursday."

Marc called Ravyn at work after he and Bruce had gone to Marc's gym and worked out. Marc even introduced him to Brent. Brent looked between Marc and Bruce.

"You two are brothers?"

Marc and Bruce looked at each other. "We are. Why?"

"You just both look so different."

"We're brothers, Brent, not twins."

"You are right. Hey, Bruce, are you a boxer like your brother?"

"I'm not. I've never boxed at all. Don't know the first thing about it."

"I'd love to show you some basic moves."

"That would be great."

Brent and Bruce moved to a corner of the gym where Brent put boxing gloves on Bruce and showed him some basic stances. Then Brent put on some boxing pads and had Bruce take some punches at him.

Bruce was tentative at first until Brent told Bruce to think of someone he wanted to beat down.

Bruce began to throw his weight into the punches he threw into Brent's pads. "Holy hell, Bruce. I'm not sure who you are thinking of but tone it down. My shoulders hurt already."

"Oh, I'm sorry. I'm sorry."

"No, I think I should call your brother over here and let him take your pounding."

"No, that's OK. We can stop."

"I hope you'll come back. I think you could be a pretty good fighter. I've been trying to get your brother to come to my boxing ring and do some sparring. Why don't you convince him to come to the ring and come with him?"

"I couldn't box like Marc."

"Well, I can pair you with someone with beginner skills like you. And you wear headgear to protect your head. I can teach you to be better if you are interested."

"I think I might like it. I liked getting my frustration out. Sorry if I hurt you. I didn't mean to."

"Don't be sorry. That's what sports creams are for."

Ravyn saw the call from Marc on her cell phone. "What's up?" she asked, trying to sound casual.

"How's Harper? Is her fever gone?"

Ravyn felt caught in her lie. "Marc, she was just being fussy. No fever this morning."

"That's wonderful. Bruce and I would like to know if we can come over for dinner tonight. We'll pick up some takeout, so you don't have to cook."

"You're coming here?"

"Is there a problem with that?"

"Of course not. I haven't cleaned the house though."

"I don't think Bruce will mind and he would like to see Blaze. He says he hopes Blaze remembers him."

"Oh sure. What time are you coming?"

"Why don't I pick up Harper, so you don't have to, and we'll see you when you get home."

Ravyn was surprised at the offer. "That would be great. I'd appreciate it."

"See you soon. Love you."

"Love you, too."

Ravyn was happy she didn't have to stop to pick up Harper that night. She was also happy she didn't have to fix dinner. She forgot to ask Marc what they were picking up.

Ravyn wondered if she should pick up some wine on the way home, then she remembered Bruce. She and Marc shouldn't drink in front of him. Instead, she stopped at the grocery store and picked up some sparkling water and some soft drinks.

She arrived home a little after six o'clock. Marc's BMW was in the driveway. She grabbed her two reusable grocery bags. She'd purchased a variety of two-liter bottles of soft drinks and a couple of liter bottles of fancy sparkling water.

"You didn't need to stop at the store, honey," Marc said, seeing her bringing in her bags. "I told you we were getting takeout."

"I got some soft drinks and some water. I wasn't sure what Bruce liked to drink, so I got cola, lemon-lime, and orange."

"I like cola. I like the orange soda, too. Usually, I like it with vodka or rum, but, well, you know."

Blaze came running up to Ravyn, wagging his tail, excited to see her.

"We'll go for a walk in a minute, Blaze. Bruce, would you like to go for a walk with us?"

"Sure. I'd like that. He's not really wanting me to pet him tonight."

"I'm sure he is just getting used to you again. Harper usually goes on the walk with us. But if the food is ready, we can eat first, then go for a walk."

"We'd better eat now before the food gets cold," Marc said.

Marc put the Thai takeout on the table. He'd gotten both brown and white rice and they filled their plates with several dishes. Marc remembered to get Ravyn's favorite chicken curry, but he'd also gotten shrimp Pad Thai, which Bruce said he liked. Marc took a little of each.

Ravyn iced down their glasses and opened the water and soft drinks.

The three of them ate slowly, making small talk. Ravyn put some rice and a few pieces of chopped-up chicken on Harper's plate. Ravyn had rinsed off the sauce. She didn't think Harper would like the curry.

When they had finished their meal, Marc said he'd clean up the table and clean up Harper. Why didn't Ravyn and Bruce walk Blaze together?

Harper saw Ravyn get the leash for Blaze and shrieked her displeasure. Harper wanted to go, too.

"I guess we'll have to clean up Harper when we get back. Our headstrong daughter wants to go, too. Why don't you come, Marc? Leave the cleaning for when we get back."

"Yeah, come with us, Marc," Bruce said.

"OK. Let me get my jacket."

The foursome and Blaze started out down the street. Ravyn had a running and walking route with Harper and Blaze, so Blaze knew the way. Ravyn had Bruce hold the leash, but Blaze wanted to run and pulled on the leash, tugging Bruce along.

"Don't let him pull you, Bruce. Jerk his leash back."

"I don't want to hurt him."

"Don't pull with all your strength. Blaze needs to know he can't run tonight."

They turned right when they got to the end of the street. The sky was clear, and the temperature was dropping.

"I wish there weren't so many streetlights, so we could see the stars," Bruce said.

"I'll take the safety of the streetlights, thank you," Marc responded.

"It's good you have a lighted leash for Blaze. It keeps him safe."

"It does. I only have one lighted vest though, but cars should be able to see us."

"We won't be out that long, will we?" Bruce asked.

"No," Ravyn said. "This is a shorter walk. This is the walk we do in the morning. In the evening, I usually run with Harper and Blaze for about three miles."

"That's a long way," Bruce said, impressed.

"It is a good walk for Blaze. Helps settle him down for the evening. And it wears Harper out too. In fact, is she asleep?"

Marc looked down into the stroller. "Looks like it."

They got back to the house. Ravyn picked up Harper, wiping her hands and face before getting her pajamas on and putting her to bed. Marc began to clean up the kitchen.

"What do you want me to do? Can I help?" Bruce asked.

"Why don't you spend a little more time with Blaze?" Ravyn suggested. "His food is in the pantry and his food bowl is on the shelf there. And be sure to give him some water. The water bowl is on the floor. Give him some fresh water. Dump out whatever is in there."

Bruce got Blaze's food out and put it in the bowl, while Blaze danced around impatiently. As soon as Bruce stepped away, Blaze began eating greedily. Bruce had put a generous amount in the bowl, not knowing how much to give Blaze.

Blaze was not going to let the opportunity go to waste and ate every bite. Bruce started to put more kibble in the bowl, but Ravyn saw what he was about to do and stopped him.

"Bruce, that's enough. He'll eat too much and get sick. Did you give him fresh water?"

"I'm doing that now."

As soon as Blaze had finished drinking fresh water, he went to his dog bed and laid down.

"Does he sleep there on his bed?"

"He does not!" Marc said. "My wife lets him sleep in my bed when I'm not home."

"Sounds like someone's jealous," Bruce teased.

"Have you seen my wife? Of course I'm jealous."

Ravyn playfully slapped Marc's arm. "Stop it."

"I guess we should think about heading back to Dunwoody," Marc said, looking at his watch.

"Wish you didn't have to."

"Why don't you come to dinner at our house tomorrow night. Can Blaze stay by himself?"

"He can. I can't stay too late, though. I'll need to walk him before I come over and then probably when I get home."

Marc pulled Ravyn in a tight hug and whispered, "Are you sure you can't sleep over?"

"I can't do that. I'd like to, but I can't."

Marc's face darkened. "I'm trying to like that dog, but I'm finding it hard. Can you bring him, and we can let him sleep out in the garage? Then he won't be in the house."

"Marc, we can't keep him out in the garage the whole time we're there. It will be too cold, and he'll get lonely."

"He gets lonely when he's home during the day."

"He has Felix for company."

"Whatever. We'll see you tomorrow for dinner, then. Without Blaze."

Soon after Marc and Bruce left her house, Ravyn texted Marc asking him to call her when he got to Dunwoody.

"What's up?" he asked after about 40 minutes.

"You and Bruce got along pretty well tonight. What happened? What's changed?" Ravyn asked.

"Let me call you back later tonight."

"OK. Love you."

"Love you, too."

Ravyn realized Bruce and Marc were probably together and Marc didn't want to speak in front of his brother.

Shortly before ten o'clock, Ravyn's cell rang.

"Hey, sorry. I was with Bruce."

"I figured you probably were. It's just, you and he seemed to be at ease with each other, and I don't think I've ever seen that between you."

"He told me what happened to him."

"Oh. I'm glad he finally told you."

"He had an episode, and then he told me. It was pretty heavy."

"An episode? What do you mean?"

"He says he has PTSD and flashbacks, to when, you know, he got attacked."

"He had a flashback?"

"Well, we were kind of fighting…"

"Fighting!" Ravyn exclaimed.

"We weren't throwing punches. He kind of grabbed me, and I grabbed him."

"Did you hurt him?" Ravyn asked, angry with her husband. "You know boxing."

"I did not hit him, I swear. And I didn't hurt him either. We both fell to the floor, and I pinned him. Then he had his flashback. He was begging me not to hurt him," Marc said with a quiver in his voice. "It was terrible. He sounded like a wounded animal."

Ravyn felt like she might cry at Bruce's hurt and pain. "What happened next?"

"He began sobbing. Hard. I've never even heard you cry that hard."

"That's because you've never been in my condo when I was alone."

"Did you cry that hard? Really? Over what?"

"Over you, dummy."

"I never knew that. I'm sorry. I'm sorry I made you cry like that."

Ravyn didn't have the nerve to tell him she'd cried that hard when they'd had a big fight and he left the house. She didn't tell him she'd cried that hard into Blaze's fur.

"Back to Bruce. Is he OK?"

"He calmed down and I got him a glass of water. Then he told me what happened. I didn't realize it was that bad. I had no idea."

"I guess you had to hear it from him."

"I guess. Then we began to talk about the past, our past, our father."

"Sounds like you had a lot to talk about."

"We did. Neither one of us could sleep last night. I'm sure we'll both sleep like the dead tonight."

"I hope you both do. What are you doing tomorrow?"

"I'm going to see if I can help him get his driver's license back."

"That's great. I'm sure you can be a big help, with your legal background and all."

"I told him, and I'll tell you, I wasn't a criminal attorney."

"No, but you understand the system. I'm glad you are going to help him."

"You know what I wish, though?"

"What?"

"And don't take this the wrong way, because I know it can never happen."

"What?"

"In that moment when we were talking about our past, I really wished we could have done it over a cold beer. Just him and me."

"Can he have non-alcoholic beer?"

"I never even thought of that. I have no idea if it tastes like the real thing. I've only ever had the real thing."

"Maybe it doesn't matter if you and he can just sit and have a beer together, like brothers everywhere in America do."

"I'll ask him about it. I don't want to make him uncomfortable."

"You realize you'll have to have that fake beer with him. You can't go and have the real thing in front of him."

"I know. I'll talk to him tomorrow. I'd better let you go, it's late and I know you have to get up in the morning. Can you take Harper to daycare? I can pick her up tomorrow evening. That way you don't have to do it all."

"That would be wonderful. Have you and Bruce gone to see your Mom?"

"We did talk to her on the phone today. We're going to visit her tomorrow, after we see what it will take to get the license back. I'm sure she'll be all dolled up for her visitors."

"Be careful. If there is a young doctor on staff, she might be getting all dolled up for him."

"God, don't even say that! I don't want a stepfather my age or younger!"

"Just teasing. Love you."

"Love you, too. Sweet dreams."

Chapter 17

Marc and Bruce awoke early the next day and both headed to the gym. Marc could put Bruce as a guest at his gym for a week. After that, he'd probably have to pay for Bruce's gym membership, if he still wanted to continue to work out at the gym chain.

Marc did leg work that morning, hitting the leg press, the hamstring curl, the hamstring press. Then he grabbed a jump rope and got his heart rate up for a little cardio.

Bruce, on the other hand, sought out Brent again and began working the exercise bag and the heavy bag. Brent recommended Bruce consider buying his own boxing gloves if he was serious about the sport. Bruce said he'd think about it, but inwardly knew he faced a big fine for his recent DUI arrest, and his job at Northside Hospital didn't pay enough for luxuries like his own boxing gloves.

The brothers headed back to their childhood home after their workout. They both showered, then Marc dropped Bruce off at Northside Hospital for work and Marc went into his office for a few hours of badly needed catchup work.

Near the end of the day, Marc picked up Harper from daycare, then fought traffic to pick up Bruce from his job. By the time they all got back to Dunwoody, Marc was exhausted. Ravyn showed up and fixed dinner.

They all spent some time together before Ravyn bundled Harper back in her SUV and headed back to their Buckhead home. Harper was sound asleep when Ravyn pulled into the driveway. She gingerly got her out of her car seat and into the house and her crib.

Tomorrow, Ravyn would remember to change Harper into her pajamas before they left Dunwoody, so she didn't have to put Harper to bed in her clothes.

Baby Steps

On Thursday morning, Bruce asked Marc if he'd go with him to a counseling session later that day.

"I really don't want to go to a group session," Marc said.

"No, this would be for just the two of us. I asked if we could have a special session."

"Why?"

"I think you and I could use some counseling together."

Marc made a face that indicated he didn't agree.

"Hear me out, Marc. You and I have been getting along pretty well, right?"

"I think so. That's why I don't think we need counseling. We're good."

"I think you are right and wrong."

"What do you mean?"

"We are getting along better, but there's still a lot of shit between us and how Dad treated us. I think a counselor can help us work through all that crap."

"I'm not so sure…"

"Please, Marc. Please do it for me. It's part of my process to stay sober."

"It's that important to you?"

"It really is."

"OK. Let me know what time the session is. But it will be just us two?"

Bruce could hardly hide his relief. "Yes, just us."

Bruce and Marc walked down a dimly lit linoleum floored corridor to enter a small office with two chairs and counselor Todd Whitehead behind his desk. The three men shook hands before Bruce and Marc sat down in older overstuffed armchairs.

"Let's just set some ground rules," Todd said. "I want you to call me Todd. And this conversation is protected by counselor-client privilege. Unless either of you has committed a serious crime, like murder or sexual assault, which by law I must report, this all will remain confidential."

Bruce and Marc nodded. "Neither one of us has committed a crime like that," Marc said, seriously. "I might have wanted to kill my brother in our youth, but as you can see, I didn't."

Bruce laughed. "I wanted to kill you plenty of times, too."

It was nervous laughter. Both brothers were ill at ease.

"Why don't we start by talking about your late father. What kind of man was he?"

"He was an asshole," Bruce interjected.

"He was a hard man to love," Marc agreed.

"Then you both had a difficult relationship with your father?" Todd asked.

"No. I had a difficult relationship with my father. Marc was the golden child. He liked Marc far more than me," Bruce said.

Marc was surprised at Bruce's vehemence. "That's not true, Bruce. He didn't like me any better."

"Are you kidding me? He loved you for becoming a lawyer like him. He told me I'd never amount to anything. He really told me that."

"Yes, Bruce, I did go into law, but that was just to please him. I hated law. I *hated* it," Marc said, standing up and beginning to pace the small office. "I felt suffocated. And I only did it to please that asshole! Once I found my passion, I wanted to start my own business and leave law. Dad was not happy. He tried to talk me out of it. Told me he wouldn't help me financially. Told me I'd fail. And, quite frankly, I was failing in my business."

Marc's shoulders slumped as he admitted that to his brother.

"But he did help you financially!" Bruce exclaimed.

"Gentlemen, this is a very constructive conversation, but let's not shout at each other. Marc, please sit down."

Marc sat back in the armchair but was agitated at Bruce's accusation that their father had favored him financially.

"Bruce, Dad did loan me money. But that was after I'd mortgaged my house for a second time. And he charged me outrageous interest because he knew he could. He was like a vulture, waiting for me to declare bankruptcy. I'd have lost my house. He really was a bastard."

"No argument there," Bruce agreed.

"I'm really sorry he cut you out of the will. He shouldn't have done that."

"It makes me feel that you think less of me because I have to depend on Mom," Bruce admitted.

"Bruce, I don't think less of you because of that. I thought less of you because of your drinking and drugs, but I didn't know the whole story. I'm hurt you didn't confide in me, quite frankly."

"Would you have believed me?"

"I'm sorry to say, I might not have. I'm glad you have confided in me now."

"So how does your father cutting Bruce out of his will make you feel, Marc?"

"I'm angry. I'm angry at my father for manipulating me and Bruce from beyond the grave. The only one who really made out is our mother and our sister. Bruce, you have to admit Brooke was the golden child. Not us."

Bruce gave a sad smile. "I guess that's right."

"How are you dealing with your grief, Marc?"

"What grief?"

"The grief over losing your father."

"I'm dealing just fine."

"Really? Your brother has told me you have been having marital difficulties."

Now Marc was angry and stood up again, his fists by his side. "Bruce, you had no right!"

Bruce put his hands up defensively. "Marc, don't hit me."

Marc unclenched his fists, then ran his right hand through his hair. "I won't hit you. I'd never hit you. You're my brother."

Suddenly, Marc put his face in his hands and began to weep. "I hated him."

Todd handed a box of facial tissues across the desk and Marc took one and sat back down.

Marc wiped his eyes and blew his nose. "I'm sorry. It's just I didn't realize how much I disliked our father. That's wrong, right?" Marc asked Todd.

"It's not wrong. It's how you feel."

Bruce was now crying, too. "I hated him, too."

Todd placed the box of tissues at the edge of his desk and Bruce wiped his eyes.

"Hate is a harsh word. You both have used it, and I respect your feelings. I'd like you to reflect on times that you had positive memories with your father, or with each other."

"I honestly can't think of a positive time with our father," Marc said. "I said he was a hard man to love, and I meant it. He was very strict. Our mother was almost his total opposite. I'll never understand how they ended up married to one another."

"Bruce, can you think of a positive memory of your father?" Todd asked.

"I can't either. Maybe we were too young to remember a positive time with him."

"Why do you say that?"

Marc broke in. "It's like he didn't like us. I mean his sons. He doted on Brooke. But with us, it was like he couldn't be bothered. No, that's not fair. He didn't pay that much attention to Brooke either."

Marc remembered Bruce saying Edward was much like him. And then he remembered Ravyn asking if he'd be unlike his father and be an attentive parent.

"I think I've failed my family," Marc said, quietly.

"What do you mean by that?" Todd asked.

"I mean, Bruce said I'm like our Dad, and I've been neglecting my own family while our mother has been ill."

"Marc, I didn't mean that," Bruce broke in.

"No, you did. And it's made me think that you were right. I need to do better for my family."

"Would you both consider another counseling session together?" Todd asked. "It sounds like you both need to work through some feelings about your father."

"I don't know…" Marc started. "I don't want this to go on forever."

"Marc, would it help if we set a limit on these sessions?" Todd asked.

"You are acting just like Dad, Marc."

Marc looked up in surprise. "OK. But I would feel better if we set a limit. Maybe in the next session, we can talk about how I can change so I'm not so much like my father."

Bruce smiled. "I think you are changing already, brother."

Marc, Bruce, and Ravyn's schedule of drop-offs and pick-ups continued for the next two weeks before Carol Linder was released from her stint at rehab. She had to walk with a walker initially when she returned home and was confined to the first floor of her house, but she then walked with a cane.

"Bruce, take care of Mom, OK?" Marc said as he packed up his things to move back to Buckhead.

"Take care of my dog," Bruce answered back.

"That dog."

"Which your wife and daughter love."

"Yes, which my wife and daughter love. Bruce, I hate to say this, but you may never get Blaze back."

"I know. But I know you are taking good care of him. I'll miss him, but I can come to visit him, right?"

"Of course! You can come often and take him for a walk and pick up after him when he poops."

"Maybe not that often."

Marc opened the front door and greeted his family as a man who had a new lease on life. Marc felt lighter and more in love. Maybe those counseling sessions were working, but he was glad he only had three more left.

Ravyn threw her arms around Marc's neck. "I'm so glad you are home for good!"

"Me, too. I've really missed you. And I'm sorry," Marc said, choking up. "I'm sorry I was so…"

Ravyn kissed him. "You were overwhelmed. I do understand. And I'm glad you are home. I've missed you, too."

"You forgive me for being such an ass?"

"I will always forgive you."

"I plan on making it up to you," Marc said.

"I can handle that."

"Baby, what time does Harper go to bed? Because we are going to bed two seconds after that and I'm going to show you how much I'm going to make it up to you and how much I've missed you," he said, wagging his eyebrows at her.

"Well, let's give Blaze and Harper an early walk and dinner, and then you and I can retire early."

"So, about Blaze. He's pretty," Marc began. He saw Ravyn's face fall. "He's pretty much ours now. Bruce just wants to visit often."

Ravyn threw her arms around Marc again, dancing with joy. "I'm so happy! I love that dog! But don't worry, I'll completely take care of him. You won't have to do anything."

"No, that's not fair. He's our dog now."

"Can I just tell you how much I'm in love with you right now?"

"You can tell me now and show me later," he said, kissing Ravyn deeply. Ravyn could feel her panties get wet and considered giving Harper some Benadryl to get her to sleep early that night. She didn't, but she thought about it.

With Harper down for the night and Blaze settled into his dog bed in Harper's room, Ravyn led Marc into the bedroom.

"Can I have another striptease?" Marc asked.

"You have time for a striptease? I'm ready to rip your clothes off right now and have my way with you."

"I love it when you talk dirty to me."

"Oh, I'll talk dirty to you, lover."

"Yeah?"

"I'll tell you how much I want to suck your dick."

"Oh, yes. I want you to do that. Suck my dick, baby."

"And how much I want you to lick my pussy."

"Oh, yes. I want to do that, too. I want to lick that kitty."

Ravyn removed her blouse and then her bra. She was trying not to be self-conscious that her formerly perky breasts now sagged a little more. She noticed Marc didn't mind. She noticed his penis was straining under his pants.

Ravyn cupped her breasts and asked, "Do you want these?"

Marc growled and removed his shirt and then his pants.

Ravyn removed her skirt and then allowed her panties to drop to the floor, kicking them across the bedroom.

Marc grabbed Ravyn. "God, I've missed you."

Ravyn just groaned and pulled Marc closer, feeling his erection against her thigh. "I need you. Right now."

"No foreplay?"

Ravyn reached down and roughly stroked his dick. Marc reached down and fingered Ravyn's clit, then put his finger inside her.

Ravyn gasped. "Inside me, now!"

They both fell onto the bed and Marc thrust his penis inside Ravyn. Ravyn bent her knees, then Marc lifted Ravyn's legs and put them on his shoulders. They both groaned their pleasure as Marc thrust deeper inside her.

Ravyn held onto Marc's arms as he stroked inside her. She could feel her orgasm beginning to form. She tried to hold it back but finally said, "Marc, I'm so close!"

"Ravyn," Marc breathed out. Then Marc tensed up and cried out his strong orgasm. Ravyn cried out her own as they both climaxed one after the other.

Marc fell on top of Ravyn, crying. Ravyn felt tears coming to her eyes, too. It was an emotional release for both of them. They panted as their ecstasy released before their breathing eased. They fell asleep blissfully in each other's arms.

Ravyn could barely wait to tell Julie that she and Marc's relationship was back on track. Ravyn was feeling confident again.

"OK, I have some news!" Ravyn said to Julie.

"I have some news, too!"

"What's your news, Julie?"

"You sure?"

"I want your news first. Do you need me to watch the girls for your next real estate exam?"

"I will, but there's a catch."

"What's the catch?"

"I reread my divorce decree."

"Why the hell would you do that?"

"I kept wondering about my alimony."

"Your alimony? Why are you worrying about that? Rob's paying it, isn't he?"

"Yes, but if I get a full-time job, he stops paying it."

"So?"

"I really need his alimony to pay for this apartment. This apartment is expensive. If I pass my real estate exam and take a full-time job with a broker, I'll lose my alimony. I still have child support."

"Don't you have money from the house, too?"

"I do. My financial planner advised me to put some of the money in CDs, an IRA for my retirement, and set up a college fund for the girls. I really can't touch any of that money right now. I have to rely on alimony, at least until early next year."

"What are you going to do?"

"I think I'm going to delay taking the exam until I'm ready. I'll need more freelance if you've got it."

"Oh my God, yes! I've got assignments I can give you today."

"If I keep my income low for now, I won't have to give up my alimony, and then I'll get my license later in the year and start my real estate career. In the meantime, I can still stage homes for sale. They pay me per house and that's really a freelance-type thing, too, so that shouldn't trigger a big income to stop the alimony."

"Is money that tight? Can I help?"

"That's really sweet of you and I love you for asking. Rob needs to pay his fair share. He divorced me. Now, what is your news?"

"I almost feel bad for telling you now. But Marc and I are good. His mother is out of rehab. Bruce is at home taking care of her and Marc is home with me. All's right with the world."

"I'm so glad for you. Are you still seeing the counselor?"

"I'm not going anymore, but Marc and Bruce have gone to a grief counselor together. They are really getting along. It makes me happy."

"What about Bruce's dog?"

"Blaze is now ours."

"How does Marc feel about that?"

"He says he's OK with it. Bruce will still come over and see his dog. Harper just loves Blaze, so I'm happy he's part of our family now."

"Only Harper loves Blaze?"

"OK, OK. I love Blaze, too. When we are out running, I feel safer. And he's turned out to be a good dog. He protects our family. He's finally stopped growling at Marc. That's a good sign."

"I'll say."

"You're really OK with waiting on your real estate license?"

"It's not forever. I'm excited to start my new career, but I can't give up my alimony right now. I need it for at least the first year of my lease."

"So, just until next December?"

"Yeah. Plus, you said you were coming to all my pool parties this summer!"

"When does the pool open?"

"Mid-May."

"We will be there!"

Ravyn hosted Bruce, Marc's mother, Julie's family, and her own family for Sunday dinner in late April. She had baked ham, sweet potato casserole, Brussel sprouts with bacon, and a mixed salad. Carol brought a mixed greens salad and Julie brought a decadent chocolate cake for dessert.

The dinner was chaotic. Harper kept feeding Blaze her ham, then cried when Ravyn scolded her to stop.

Marc had purchased non-alcoholic beer for him and Bruce to drink, but Ravyn also bought sparkling cider, which Bruce had instead. "That fake beer tastes terrible," Bruce said.

Marc took one swig and agreed. His bottle got dumped down the drain and he opted for a wine Julie had brought.

They all raised their glasses.

There was laughter around the table before they all decided to take a nice walk around the neighborhood with Blaze.

"Go!" Harper kept commanding as she sat in her stroller. She kicked her feet, willing everyone to speed up. Then she put her arms up, wanting to get out of the stroller to walk with everyone.

"She's getting so independent and headstrong," Ravyn said, as she lifted Harper out and stood her on her feet. Harper still needed to hold onto the stroller, but seemed happier walking, until she got just a few yards and wanted back in the stroller.

"It's like this when we go for our walks now," she told Julie. "She wants in, then out, then back in her stroller. It's taking me much longer to walk the dog in the afternoons if she comes. And she insists on coming for the walk. In the morning, I can just take Blaze and we can run."

"Independent and headstrong, huh? Takes after her mother if you ask me," Marc teased.

"So how are you doing with your real estate license?" Ravyn asked Julie. "Have you scheduled another exam date?"

"I haven't yet," she admitted. "But I've been so busy staging houses. I've been doing it for one agency, but another agency wants to hire me as well! I just need make sure I don't make too much and lose my alimony. I really need it to pay my rent. I'm going to talk to a CPA about it."

"I don't suppose you can renegotiate it with Rob?"

"Absolutely not. We barely speak now. We text each other and he picks up the girls from school on Friday on the weekends he has them. Then he drops them off on Monday, so I never have to see his ugly mug."

"I'm sorry it's that bad," Ravyn said.

"It's really bad, but the girls tell me Rob and his new wife aren't doing so well, either."

"They're not? That was fast."

"Tell me about it. The girls have heard them fighting when they are with him."

"That's not good."

"The girls tell me they are fighting about money," Julie said. "I think that homewrecker was expecting to marry the Rob who can spend lavishly on her. You know, the Rob before the divorce. After the divorce, he can't. He's not broke, but he's not the money man she thought he was. The divorce was expensive enough for me, but he had to buy me out of that house. He's basically poor. I know it's wrong of me, I'm not unhappy that he's unhappy."

"What does that mean for you?"

"It means I can't do anything that will give him a reason to stop paying me alimony," she said. "If that means I need to put a hold on my real estate license, then so be it. I'm keeping busy with staging houses right now. Spring is one of the busiest times for home sales."

"You are just delaying your dream?"

"Just delayed. It gives me more time to study. And I honestly love staging houses. I hope it will help me be a better real estate agent in the end."

"I know it will. I'm excited for you."

The group returned home, where Carol and Julie's daughters had stayed behind. Carol had graduated to walking without a cane, but she said a walk around the neighborhood would tire her too much, and she wanted to visit a while longer.

About an hour later, Carol said she was ready to go home. After hugs all around, Bruce led his mother out to his late father's Lexus and helped her into the passenger's side.

"Bruce got his driver's license back?" Julie asked Ravyn as they stood at the front door. Julie's daughters scrambled to her car, Lexie yelling "Shotgun!" leading to an argument between the sisters.

"Marc helped him get it back," she answered.

"They are getting along?"

"They are. Marc goes to the Dunwoody gym on the weekends, and they work out together. Bruce and Carol come over for dinner once a week and we go there once a week too. I'm really glad they are getting along."

"I'm happy for both of them," Julie said. "And you guys are doing OK?"

"I'm very happy we are doing OK, too."

"Are you back on the pill?"

"Not yet. I've made an appointment with my doctor. She wants to see me before I go back on it."

"You know I hate to ask this, but are you and Marc using protection?"

Ravyn frowned. "We are not. But I'm not pregnant. I took that test when you scared me."

"Ravyn, how long ago was that? Two months ago? Three?"

"Julie, don't scare me again. I'm not pregnant. My periods are regular."

"As long as you're sure."

"I'm sure," Ravyn said, hugging her friend. "Thanks for coming today. I can't believe how big the girls are getting."

"Yeah. I know they stayed on their iPads a lot while we were here. I told them they couldn't have them at the table, so they were a bit miffed at me. When Rob has the girls, they tell me he lets them use them at the dinner table."

"Really? That's awful."

"He makes me out to be the bad parent when I put my foot down when he's really the shitty parent."

Ravyn made a face and said, "Eek. You are the parent. Rob sounds like a child."

"He is a child. I am glad to be rid of him."

The friends hugged again, and Ashley and Lexie just honked the car horn to let their mother know they were ready to go.

"Guess that's your signal."

Julie rolled her eyes before waving goodbye to her friend. "Don't let Harper become a teenager!"

Ravyn laughed before closing the front door.

Chapter 18

Ravyn sat in her OB/GYN's office. Dr. Watkins was asking Ravyn about her nutrition and how she was feeling.

"I'm feeling good. I have a new dog and we go for runs in the morning. But I'm ready to be back on the pill."

"Have you and your husband been having protected sex?"

"No. He's not wild about condoms and neither am I."

Dr. Watkins frowned. "I think we better give you a pregnancy test before I write the prescription. And after this appointment, you can return to your primary care physician."

"I'm not pregnant. I'd know."

"You didn't know the first time," her doctor cautioned.

"Listen, I am planning my pregnancies from now on," Ravyn said.

"Fair enough."

Dr. Watkins drew Ravyn's blood and stepped out of the exam room.

Ravyn suddenly felt nervous. She took deep breaths, trying not to panic. I am not pregnant, she chanted to herself. I am not pregnant. I am not pregnant.

Dr. Watkins returned to the exam room.

"Ravyn, I'm sorry to say I can't prescribe birth control for you. You're pregnant."

Ravyn burst into tears.

Marc got home to find Ravyn had been crying.

"What's wrong?"

"We're pregnant again!"

"What? Weren't you going back on the pill?"

"That's why I went to the doctor, to get back on it. I didn't get on it in time. And we weren't careful."

"Oh, shit. I guess I should have…"

"We both should have."

"Are we ready?"

"Too late to ask that now!" Ravyn said. "This better be the last one, though."

"OK," Marc said quietly. "It's your body and if you say this is it, I'll get a vasectomy after the baby is born."

"Do you care what it is?"

"I'd be lying if I said I just want it to be healthy. I do want it to be healthy, but I hope it's a boy. A son. Is that selfish of me?"

"No, I'm hoping it's a boy too. I'd like one of each."

"Are we going to find out the gender?"

"I think we should. Then we can decide on a name right away."

"Well, I know what name it won't be if it's a boy," Marc said. "Edward. I am not naming my son after that man."

"Marc, we're getting ahead of ourselves. We don't know if it's a boy yet. We may be picking out girl's names again."

"When are you due?"

"It's a guess, but they think I'm actually five weeks along. But I swear I had a period! I really didn't think I was pregnant."

"Can that happen? A period, I mean?"

"Apparently some women can have a light period when they are early in their pregnancy. I guess I'm one of those women."

"When are you due?"

"Sometime after Christmas," she answered. "Mid-January, maybe."

"Another baby," Marc said, hugging his wife. Marc looked around his house. "You know, we might want to think about a bigger house. We just paid off that second mortgage so we could probably swing selling this house and buying something bigger."

"No, Marc! I love this house!"

"But we'll need another bedroom if we want to have guests come to stay."

"Can we do an addition?"

"Maybe. I'll have to take out a second mortgage again to pay for that. Are you willing to stick with me until that's paid off?"

"Marc, with two kids, a cat, and a dog, you'll never get rid of me."

"That's what I want to hear. We're in this together."

Renovation on Marc and Ravyn's house started in early September. With all the banging and dust, Ravyn considered moving into a hotel, but the contractors put up a wooden barrier as they built an extra bedroom and bathroom on what used to be the patio.

Baby Steps

Marc and Ravyn had plans to move the patio behind the new addition. They didn't want to give up their fire pit, but now it would be hidden from their neighbors Eleanor and Arthur Carter. They doubted they would be able to see it and accidentally call the fire department on them.

The upside to the addition and the movement of the back patio was their backyard would be much smaller. Less mowing for Marc. He joked he could now do it with a weed eater.

They also cleaned out the garage, putting some furniture into storage for Bruce when he finally got his own apartment. They sold or donated the rest.

Cleaning out the garage meant Marc's car and Ravyn's SUV would finally fit inside. With the new baby coming, Marc realized he'd need a bigger vehicle than his old BMW.

Marc opted for a black Jeep Wrangler. If he was going to drive his children around, he was going to drive them in the most masculine vehicle he could find. His Jeep Wrangler did sport a "Baby on Board" sticker, however.

Ravyn felt like she'd gained more weight with this baby than with Harper, but she was right on track with her pregnancy. Even Dr. Watkins said it was unlikely Ravyn would go on bed rest with this pregnancy unless it was medically necessary. Ravyn was relieved to learn that news.

She and Marc were delighted when an ultrasound showed they were having a boy this time.

Ravyn smiled as she rubbed her belly as she and her daughter lay on the couch. "Harper, you're going to be a big sister."

Harper rubbed her mother's belly, too. She felt the baby kick and her eyes got big.

"Did you feel your brother kick?" Ravyn asked. Harper nodded.

Harper was talking more now. She had graduated from calling Blaze "baas" to calling him "bees." She pointed to Ravyn's belly and said "Baby?"

"Yes. Mommy's having a baby. Your baby brother."

Ravyn was frustrated that she and Marc could not agree on a name for their future son. Ravyn thought they could name him after her father's middle name, Samuel, but Marc didn't like that name.

"Why not?"

"I just don't like it."

"I could see if it was an old boyfriend of mine, but I never dated a Samuel," Ravyn teased.

"I never even thought about that. What men's names have you dated? Because those are now off the list."

"What names do you like? We can start there. But I get to veto it if I don't like the name."

"What about Liam? Liam Linder."

"Liam? Like Liam Neeson? The actor? You've been watching too many movies."

"I like Liam."

"Let's think about it. It sounds a little too alliterative. Liam Linder."

"We could give him a middle name. Liam Shaw Linder."

"We don't need to give him my maiden name."

"We don't?"

"Not necessarily. We could give him another middle name. Like Samuel."

"Ravyn, you are trying to sneak that name in. I said no to Samuel."

"Is Linder an Irish surname?"

"Nope. It's Swedish."

"Swedish? I married a Swede?"

"What do you have against the Swedes?"

"Nothing. I just thought as a Swede you'd be blond and blue-eyed and really like ABBA."

"Are you sorry I'm not blond and blue-eyed?"

"No sir. I love those hazel eyes of yours."

"What is the Shaw surname?" Marc asked.

"English. Which is why I ended up with the name Ravyn."

"I love your name. I've never known another woman by that name."

"I'm sure you never will either."

"What about Liam?"

"Let me think about it. I just think he will need a middle name."

"What about Oliver?" Marc asked. "Liam Oliver Linder has a nice ring to it."

"You realize his initials will be LOL. I can't have my son with emoji initials." Marc laughed. "I didn't think of that."

"What about Daniel? Would you consider Daniel as his first name?"

"Maybe. Daniel Liam Linder," Marc said, sounding out the name. "Any issue with the initials DLL?"

"Not really."

"We might have a name for our son."

"Daniel Liam Linder. Let's sleep on it. We agreed so easily on Harper's name. Why is agreeing on our son's name so much harder?"

"We do have a little more than four months before we have to decide."

"Daniel Liam Linder. Sounds like a good name for a lawyer," Ravyn teased.

Marc rolled his eyes. "If Daniel wants to go into law, that's fine. But it has to be his idea, his passion."

"What if Harper wants to go to law school?"

"That daughter of mine can, and will, do whatever she wants. I know she's not two yet, but my God she's so stubborn."

"She is almost 18 months. I guess that's close enough to the terrible twos. Ugh! I can't believe I'm going to have two children in diapers! I really wanted to space them out."

"We should invest in whoever makes diapers."

"That's not funny."

"I promise you I'll take care of it. No more unexpected pregnancies. We're good with two, right?"

"I think so."

"Honey, you need to be sure. I'm not going to get snipped if you think you want more."

"I've got four months to think about it."

The families gathered at Carol's house for Thanksgiving. Carol had healed from her broken hip and wrist and moved slowly around the kitchen while Ravyn sat on a stool uncomfortable and unable to help with preparations.

"I feel like I'm about to pop," Ravyn admitted. "I know it won't be too long now, but I'm getting anxious to meet my son."

"I'm excited to meet my grandson! I know I have one grandson already, but he's out in Phoenix. I don't get to see him grow up. It will be nice to have another grandchild closer that I get to spoil, like I do your daughter."

"I'm just praying Harper will take a nap today. With all the excitement, she may not. She's so strong-willed," Ravyn said, shifting uncomfortably on the stool.

"Why don't I pull in a dining room chair? That will be more comfortable for you to sit on. Marc! Bruce! Pull a chair in here for Ravyn."

Bruce brought a chair from the dining room where Carol had laid out a formal table. She had gotten out her wedding china and crystal for the holiday meal. She thought she should use it whenever she could.

"Thank you, Bruce," his mother said and turned to Ravyn. "Now sit."

"Thanks. It's hard to stand. It's hard to sit. It's hard to sleep. And I've had the worst heartburn. I practically have to sleep sitting up."

"Well, I hope for your sake it's over soon."

"Me, too."

The family sat around the dining room table, passing around turkey, mashed potatoes, gravy and all the other traditional fixings. Carol served sparkling cider in the crystal wine glasses. Everyone at the table was practicing sobriety, whether forced, like Ravyn, or by choice, like Bruce and Marc.

Marc had decided to practice sympathetic sobriety for his wife's second pregnancy and was surprised that once he gave up his nightly scotch, how much better he felt in the morning.

"Marc, how are you doing without alcohol?" Bruce asked.

"I was surprised that it was hard at first, but I feel great now," his brother responded. "And I've lost some weight."

"I know what you mean. There are times it's difficult for me, but then I call my sponsor," Bruce said. "He keeps telling me it takes baby steps. They may be a little wobbly, but it's still baby steps."

"Bruce, that's how all life is. We're all taking baby steps forward," Ravyn said, raising her glass of cider. "To baby steps."

Made in United States
Troutdale, OR
08/04/2024